Blithe Spirit

An Improbable Farce
in Three Acts

Noël Coward

A SAMUEL FRENCH ACTING EDITION

SAMUEL FRENCH
FOUNDED 1830

SAMUELFRENCH.COM
SAMUELFRENCH-LONDON.CO.UK

MUSIC USE NOTE

IMPORTANT BILLING AND CREDIT REQUIREMENTS

BLITHE SPIRIT was produced by John C. Wilson at the Morosco Theatre in New York. The play was directed by Mr. Wilson, the setting was designed by Stewart Chaney and the cast was as follows:

EDITH	Jacqueline Clark
RUTH	Peggy Wood
CHARLES	Clifton Webb
DR. BRADMAN	Philip Tonge
MRS. BRADMAN	Phyllis Joyce
MADAME ARCATI	Mildred Natwick
ELVIRA	Leonora Corbett

The action of the play passes in the living-room of Charles Condomine's house in Kent.

SYNOPSIS OF SCENES

ACT I

SCENE 1.—Before dinner on a summer evening.
SCENE 2.—After dinner.

ACT II

SCENE 1.—The next morning.
SCENE 2.—Late the following afternoon.
SCENE 3.—Early evening. A few days later.

ACT III

SCENE 1.—After dinner. A few days later.
SCENE 2.—Several hours later.

iii

BLITHE SPIRIT

Produced at the Opera House, Manchester, on June 16th, 1941, and then played at the Piccadilly Theatre, London, on July 2nd, 1941, with the following cast of characters:

EDITH (a Maid)	Ruth Reeves.
RUTH	Fay Compton.
CHARLES	Cecil Parker.
DOCTOR BRADMAN	Martin Lewis.
MRS. BRADMAN	Moya Nugent.
MADAME ARCATI	Margaret Rutherford.
ELVIRA	Kay Hammond.

BLITHE SPIRIT

ACT I

Scene i

The Scene is the living-room of the Condomines' house in Kent. The room is light, attractive and comfortably furnished. On the L there are french windows opening on to the garden. On the R there is an open fireplace. At the back there are double doors leading to the hall, the dining-room, the stairs, and the servants' quarters.

Light Cue No. 1, Act I, Scene 1.

When the Curtain rises it is about eight o'clock on a summer evening. There is a wood fire burning because it is an English summer evening. The doors are open, the windows are closed. The curtains are partially closed.

Edith comes in from the hall carrying, rather uneasily, a large tray of cocktail things. She comes to the c table with the tray of drinks. She sees there is no room, so puts it on the drinks table up stage R with a sigh of relief.

Ruth enters c briskly. She is a smart-looking woman in the middle thirties. She is dressed for dinner, but not elaborately.

Ruth. That's right, Edith.

Edith. Yes'm.

Ruth. Now you'd better fetch the ice-bucket.

Edith. Yes'm.

Ruth (*arranging the ornaments on the piano*) Did you manage to get the ice out of those little tin trays?

Edith. Yes'm—I 'ad a bit of a struggle though—but it's all right.

Ruth. And you filled the little trays up again with water?

Edith. Yes'm.

Ruth (*moving to the window and arranging the curtains*) Very good, Edith—you're making giant strides.

Edith. Yes'm.

Ruth. Madame Arcati, Mrs Bradman and I will have our coffee in here after dinner, and Mr Condomine and Doctor Bradman will have theirs in the dining-room—is that quite clear?

Edith. Yes'm.

Ruth. And when you're serving dinner, Edith, try to remember to do it calmly and methodically.

Edith. Yes'm.

Ruth. As you are not in the Navy, it is unnecessary to do everything at the double.

EDITH. Very good, 'm.

RUTH. Now go and get the ice.

EDITH (*straining at the leash*) Yes'm. (*She starts off at full speed*)

RUTH. *Not* at a run, Edith.

EDITH (*slowing down*) Yes'm.

(EDITH goes)

RUTH *crosses to the fireplace and then gives a comprehensive glance round the room.*

CHARLES *comes in* C *and moves to the back of the sofa. He is a nice-looking man of about forty, wearing a loose-fitting velvet smoking-jacket*)

CHARLES. No sign of the advancing hordes?

RUTH. Not yet.

CHARLES (*moving to the drinks table; going to the cocktail tray*) No ice.

RUTH. It's coming. I've been trying to discourage Edith from being quite so fleet of foot. You mustn't mind if everything is a little slow motion to-night.

CHARLES (*coming to* L *of Ruth, above the sofa*) I shall welcome it. The last few days have been extremely agitating. What do you suppose induced Agnes to leave us and go and get married?

RUTH. The reason was becoming increasingly obvious, dear.

CHARLES. Yes, but in these days nobody thinks anything of that sort of thing. She could have popped into the cottage hospital, had it, and popped out again.

RUTH. Her social life would have been seriously undermined.

CHARLES (*moving to the drinks table again*) We must keep Edith in the house more.

(EDITH *comes in slowly with the ice-bucket*)

RUTH. That's right, Edith. Put it down on the table.

EDITH (*putting the ice-bucket on the drinks table—up stage* R) Yes'm.

CHARLES. I left my cigarette-case on my dressing-table, Edith. Would you get it for me?

EDITH. Yes, sir.

(EDITH *runs out of the room*)

CHARLES. There now!

RUTH. You took her by surprise.

CHARLES (*at the cocktail table*) A dry Martini, I think, don't you?

(RUTH *takes a cigarette from the box on the mantelpiece and lights it, then she crosses and sits in the armchair.* CHARLES *is mixing cocktails*)

RUTH. Yes, darling. I expect Madame Arcati will want something sweeter.

CHARLES. We'll have this one for ourselves, anyhow.

RUTH. Oh dear!

CHARLES. What's the matter?

RUTH. I have a feeling that this evening's going to be awful.

CHARLES. It'll probably be funny, but not awful.

RUTH. You must promise not to catch my eye. If I giggle—and I'm very likely to—it will ruin everything.

CHARLES. You mustn't. You must be dead serious and if possible a little intense. We can't hurt the old girl's feelings, however funny she is.

RUTH. But why the Bradmans, darling? He's as sceptical as we are. He'll probably say the most dreadful things.

CHARLES. I've warned him. There must be more than three people and we couldn't have the Vicar and his wife because (a) they're dreary, and (b) they probably wouldn't have approved at all. It had to be the Bradmans.

(EDITH *rushes into the room with Charles's cigarette-case*)

(*Taking it*) Thank you, Edith. Steady does it.

EDITH (*breathlessly*) Yes, sir.

(EDITH, *with an obvious effort, goes out slowly*)

CHARLES. We might make her walk about with a book on her head like they do in deportment lessons.

(CHARLES *comes to* R *of Ruth and gives her a cocktail. Then he moves to the fireplace*)

Here, try this.

RUTH (*sipping it*) Lovely—dry as a bone.

CHARLES (*raising his glass to her*) To 'The Unseen'!

RUTH. I must say that's a wonderful title.

CHARLES. If this evening's a success, I shall start on the first draft tomorrow.

RUTH. How extraordinary it is.

CHARLES. What?

RUTH. Oh, I don't know—being right at the beginning of something. It gives one an odd feeling.

CHARLES (*at the fireplace, facing Ruth*) Do you remember how I got the idea for *The Light Goes Out?*

RUTH. Suddenly seeing that haggard, raddled woman in the hotel at Biarritz. Of course I remember. We sat up half the night talking about it.

CHARLES. She certainly came in very handy. I wonder who she was.

RUTH. And if she ever knew, I mean ever recognized, that description of herself. Poor thing . . . here's to her, anyhow. (*She finishes her drink*)

CHARLES (*going to her, taking her glass and moving up to the drinks table*) Have another.

RUTH. Darling—it's most awfully strong.

CHARLES (*pouring it*) Never mind.

RUTH. Used Elvira to be a help to you—when you were thinking something out, I mean?

CHARLES (*pouring out another cocktail for himself*) Every now and then—when she concentrated—but she didn't concentrate very often.

RUTH. I do wish I'd known her.

CHARLES. I wonder if you'd have liked her.

RUTH. I'm sure I should. As you talk of her she sounds enchanting. Yes, I'm sure I should have liked her because you know I have never for an instant felt in the least jealous of her. That's a good sign.

CHARLES. Poor Elvira. (*He comes to the L of Ruth and gives her a cocktail*)

RUTH. Does it still hurt? When you think of her?

CHARLES. No, not really. Sometimes I almost wish it did. I feel rather guilty . . .

RUTH. I wonder if I died before you'd grown tired of me if you'd forget me so soon?

CHARLES. What a horrible thing to say.

RUTH. No, I think it's interesting.

CHARLES (*crossing below Ruth and sitting on the left end of the sofa*) Well, to begin with, I haven't forgotten Elvira. I remember her very distinctly indeed. I remember how fascinating she was, and how maddening. I remember how badly she played all games and how cross she got when she didn't win. I remember her gay charm when she had achieved her own way over something and her extreme acidity when she didn't. I remember her physical attractiveness, which was tremendous, and her spiritual integrity, which was nil.

RUTH. You can't remember something that was nil.

CHARLES. I remember how morally untidy she was.

RUTH. Was she more physically attractive than I am?

CHARLES. That was a very tiresome question, dear, and fully deserves the wrong answer.

RUTH. You really are very sweet.

CHARLES. Thank you.

RUTH. And a little naïve, too.

CHARLES. Why?

RUTH. Because you imagine that I mind about Elvira being more physically attractive than I am.

CHARLES. I should have thought any woman would mind—if it were true. Or perhaps I'm old-fashioned in my view of female psychology.

RUTH. Not exactly old-fashioned, darling, just a bit didactic.

CHARLES. How do you mean?

RUTH. It's didactic to attribute to one type the defects of

another type. For instance, because you know perfectly well that
Elvira would mind terribly if you found another woman more
attractive physically than she was, it doesn't necessarily follow
that I should. Elvira was a more physical person than I. I'm
certain of that. It's all a question of degree.

CHARLES (*smiling*) I love you, my love.

RUTH. I know you do; but not the wildest stretch of imagina-
tion could describe it as the first fine careless rapture.

CHARLES. Would you like it to be?

RUTH. Good God, no!

CHARLES. Wasn't that a shade too vehement?

RUTH. We're neither of us adolescent, Charles; we've neither of
us led exactly prim lives, have we? And we've both been married
before. Careless rapture at this stage would be incongruous and
embarrassing.

CHARLES. I hope I haven't been in any way a disappointment,
dear.

RUTH. Don't be so idiotic.

CHARLES. After all, your first husband was a great deal older
than you, wasn't he? I shouldn't like you to think that you'd
missed out all along the line.

RUTH. There are moments, Charles, when you go too far.

CHARLES. Sorry, darling.

RUTH. As far as waspish female psychology goes, there's a
rather strong vein of it in you.

CHARLES. I've heard that said about Julius Cæsar.

RUTH. Julius Cæsar is neither here nor there.

CHARLES. He may be for all we know. We'll ask Madame
Arcati.

RUTH (*rising and crossing to* L) You're awfully irritating when
you're determined to be witty at all costs, almost supercilious.

CHARLES. That's exactly what Elvira used to say.

RUTH. I'm not at all surprised. I never imagined, physically
triumphant as she was, that she was entirely lacking in perception.

(CHARLES *rises and goes to the* R *of Ruth*)

CHARLES. Darling Ruth!

RUTH. There you go again!

CHARLES (*kissing her lightly*) As I think I mentioned before, I
love you, my love.

RUTH. Poor Elvira!

CHARLES. Didn't that light, comradely kiss mollify you at all?

RUTH. You're very annoying, you know you are. When I said
'Poor Elvira' it came from the heart. You must have bewildered
her so horribly.

CHARLES. Don't I ever bewilder you at all?

RUTH. Never for an instant. I know every trick.

CHARLES. Well, all I can say is that we'd better get a divorce immediately.

RUTH. Put my glass down, there's a darling.

CHARLES (*taking it*) She certainly had a great talent for living. It was a pity that she died so young.

RUTH. Poor Elvira!

CHARLES (*crossing to and putting the glasses on the drinks table*) That remark is getting monotonous.

RUTH (*moving up stage a pace*) Poor Charles, then.

CHARLES. That's better.

RUTH. And later on, poor Ruth, I expect.

CHARLES (*coming to above the c table*) You have no faith, Ruth. I really do think you should try to have a little faith.

RUTH (*moving to the L arm of the armchair*) I shall strain every nerve.

CHARLES. Life without faith is an arid business.

RUTH. How beautifully you put things, dear.

CHARLES. I aim to please.

RUTH. If I died, I wonder how long it would be before you married again?

CHARLES. You won't die. You're not the dying sort.

RUTH. Neither was Elvira.

CHARLES. Oh yes, she was, now that I look back on it. She had a certain ethereal, not-quite-of-this-world quality. Nobody could call you, even remotely, ethereal.

(RUTH *crosses below the sofa to the fire.* CHARLES *moves to the armchair*)

RUTH. Nonsense! She was of the earth, earthy.

CHARLES. Well, she is now, anyhow.

RUTH. You know that's the kind of observation that shocks people.

CHARLES. It's discouraging to think how many people are shocked by honesty and how few by deceit.

RUTH. Write that down; you might forget it.

CHARLES. You underrate me.

RUTH. Anyhow, it was a question of bad taste more than honesty.

CHARLES (*moving to below the sofa*) I was devoted to Elvira. We were married for five years. She died. I missed her very much. (*He comes to Ruth, pats her cheek, and then goes back to the armchair*) That was seven years ago. I have now—with your help, my love—risen above the whole thing.

RUTH. Admirable. But if tragedy should darken our lives, I still say—with prophetic foreboding—poor Ruth!

(*A bell is heard*)

CHARLES. That's probably the Bradmans.

RUTH. It might be Madame Arcati.

CHARLES. No, she'll come on her bicycle. She always goes everywhere on her bicycle.

RUTH. It really is very spirited of the old girl.

CHARLES. Shall I go, or shall we let Edith have her fling? (*He moves L to below the piano*)

RUTH. Wait a minute and see what happens.

(*There is a slight pause*)

CHARLES. Perhaps she didn't hear.

RUTH. She's probably on one knee in a pre-sprinting position, waiting for cook to open the kitchen door.

(*There is the sound of a door banging and* EDITH *is seen scampering across the hall*)

CHARLES. Steady, Edith.

EDITH (*dropping to a walk*) Yes, sir.

(*After a moment,* DR *and* MRS BRADMAN *come into the room.* CHARLES *goes forward to meet them. Dr Bradman is a pleasant-looking middle-aged man. Mrs Bradman is fair and rather faded.* MRS BRADMAN *comes to* RUTH, *who meets her above the sofa and shakes hands.* DR BRADMAN *shakes hands with* CHARLES)

Doctor and Mrs Bradman.

(EDITH *goes*)

DR BRADMAN. We're not late, are we? I only got back from the hospital about half an hour ago.

CHARLES. Of course not. Madame Arcati isn't here yet.

MRS BRADMAN. That must have been her we passed coming down the hill. I said I thought it was.

RUTH. Then she won't be long. I'm so glad you were able to come.

(RUTH *comes down on the* R *of the sofa and sits on the pouffe.* MRS BRADMAN *sits on the* R *end of the sofa*)

MRS BRADMAN. We've been looking forward to it. I feel really quite excited.

DR BRADMAN (*moving to above the sofa and standing behind Mrs Bradman*) I guarantee that Violet will be good. I made her promise.

MRS BRADMAN. There wasn't any need. I'm absolutely thrilled. I've only seen Madame Arcati two or three times in the village. I mean I've never seen her do anything at all peculiar, if you know what I mean?

CHARLES. Dry Martini?

DR BRADMAN. By all means.

(CHARLES *goes up to the drinks table and starts mixing fresh cocktails.* DR BRADMAN *goes up and stands by Charles*)

CHARLES (*mixing*) She certainly is a strange woman. It was only a chance remark of the Vicar's about seeing her up on the Knoll on Midsummer Eve dressed in sort of Indian robes that made me realize that she was psychic at all. Then I began to make enquiries. Apparently she's been a professional in London for years.

MRS BRADMAN. It is funny, isn't it? I mean anybody doing it as a profession.

DR BRADMAN (*sitting on the back of the sofa*) I believe it's very lucrative.

MRS BRADMAN. Do you believe in it, Mrs Condomine? Do you think there's anything really genuine about it at all?

RUTH. I'm afraid not; but I do think it's interesting how easily people allow themselves to be deceived.

MRS BRADMAN. But she must believe it herself, mustn't she? Or is the whole business a fake?

CHARLES. I suspect the worst. A real professional charlatan. That's what I am hoping for, anyhow. The character I am planning for my book must be a complete impostor. That's one of the most important factors of the whole story.

DR BRADMAN. What exactly are you hoping to get from her?

CHARLES. Jargon, principally; a few of the tricks of the trade. I haven't been to a séance for years. I want to refresh my memory.

DR BRADMAN (*rising*) Then it's not entirely new to you?

CHARLES (*handing drinks to Dr and Mrs Bradman; above the sofa*) Oh, no. When I was a little boy an aunt of mine used to come and stay with us. She imagined that she was a medium and used to go off into the most elaborate trances after dinner. My mother was fascinated by it.

MRS BRADMAN. Was she convinced?

CHARLES. Good heavens, no. She just naturally disliked my aunt and loved making a fool of her. (*He gets a cocktail for himself and then comes to above the c table*)

DR BRADMAN (*laughing*) I gather that there were never any tangible results?

CHARLES. Oh, sometimes she didn't do so badly. On one occasion when we were all sitting round in the pitch dark with my mother groping her way through Chaminade at the piano, my aunt suddenly gave a shrill scream and said that she saw a small black dog by my chair. Then someone switched on the lights and sure enough there it was.

MRS BRADMAN. But how extraordinary.

CHARLES. It was obviously a stray that had come in from the street. But I must say I took off my hat to Auntie for producing it, or rather for utilizing it. Even Mother was a bit shaken.

MRS BRADMAN. What happened to it?

CHARLES. It lived with us for years.

RUTH. I sincerely hope Madame Arcati won't produce any livestock. We have so very little room in this house.

Mrs Bradman. Do you think she tells fortunes? I love having my fortune told.

Charles. I expect so.

Ruth. I was told once on the pier at Southsea that I was surrounded by lilies and a golden seven. It worried me for days.

(*They all laugh*)

Charles. We really must all be serious, you know, and pretend that we believe implicitly. Otherwise she won't play.

Ruth. Also, she might really mind. It would be cruel to upset her.

Dr Bradman. I shall be as good as gold.

Ruth. Have you ever attended her, Doctor—professionally, I mean.

Dr Bradman. Yes. She had influenza in January. She's only been here just over a year, you know. I must say she was singularly unpsychic then. I always understood that she was an authoress.

Charles. Oh yes. We originally met as colleagues at one of Mrs Wilmot's Sunday evenings in Sandgate.

Mrs Bradman. What sort of books does she write?

Charles. Two sorts. Rather whimsical children's stories about enchanted woods filled with highly conventional flora and fauna; and enthusiastic biographies of minor royalties, very sentimental, reverent and extremely funny.

(*There is the sound of the front-door bell*)

Ruth. Here she is.

Dr Bradman. She knows, doesn't she, about tonight? You're not going to spring it on her.

Charles. Of course. It was all arranged last week. I told her how profoundly interested I was in anything to do with the occult, and she blossomed like a rose.

Ruth. I really feel quite nervous; as though I were going to make a speech.

(*Edith is seen sedately going towards the door*)

Charles. You go and meet her, darling.

(*Ruth crosses up stage to the r side of the door. Charles to the l side of the door by the piano. Dr Bradman moves to above the sofa. Meanwhile Edith has opened the door, and Madame Arcati's voice, very high and clear, is heard*)

Madame Arcati (*off*) I've leant my bike up against that little bush; it will be *perfectly* all right if no one touches it.

Edith (*appearing*) Madame Arcati.

Ruth. How nice of you to have come all this way.

(*Madame Arcati enters. She is a striking woman, dressed not too extravagantly but with a decided bias towards the barbaric. She might be any age between forty-five and sixty-five.* RUTH *ushers her in.* RUTH *and* CHARLES *greet her simultaneously)*

CHARLES. My dear Madame Arcati!

MADAME ARCATI. I'm afraid I'm rather late; but I had a sudden presentiment that I was going to have a puncture so I went back to fetch my pump.

(MADAME ARCATI *takes off her cloak and hands it to* RUTH, *who puts it on the chair* R *of the door)*

And then, of course, I didn't have a puncture at all.

CHARLES. Perhaps you will on the way home.

MADAME ARCATI (*moving below Ruth to* R *to shake hands with* DR BRADMAN. *Greeting him*) Doctor Bradman—the man with the gentle hands!

DR BRADMAN. I'm delighted to see you looking so well. This is my wife.

(MADAME ARCATI *shakes hands with* MRS BRADMAN *over the back of the sofa.* DR BRADMAN *moves to the fireplace)*

MADAME ARCATI. We are old friends—we meet coming out of shops.

CHARLES. Would you like a cocktail?

MADAME ARCATI (*peeling off some rather strange-looking gloves*) If it's a dry Martini, yes—if it's a concoction, no. Experience has taught me to be very wary of concoctions.

CHARLES (*up to the drinks table*) It is a dry Martini.

(MADAME ARCATI *moves to Ruth,* C)

MADAME ARCATI. How delicious. It was wonderful cycling through the woods this evening. I was deafened with bird song.

RUTH. It's been lovely all day.

MADAME ARCATI. But the evening's the time—mark my words. (*She takes the cocktail* CHARLES *gives her, he having come down on her* R) Thank you. Cheers! Cheers!

(RUTH *leads* MADAME ARCATI *down stage to the* L *end of the sofa, where she sits.* RUTH *sits on the right arm of the armchair.* DR BRADMAN *is at the fireplace.* CHARLES *is above the* C *table)*

RUTH. Don't you find it very tiring bicycling everywhere?

MADAME ARCATI. On the contrary, it stimulates me. I was getting far too sedentary in London. That horrid little flat with dim lights! They had to be dim, you know; the clients expect it.

MRS BRADMAN. I must say I find bicycling very exhausting.

MADAME ARCATI. Steady rhythm, that's what counts. Once you get the knack of it you need never look back. On you get and away you go.

MRS BRADMAN. But the hills, Madame Arcati; pushing up those awful hills.

MADAME ARCATI. Just knack again. Down with your head, up with your heart, and you're over the top like a flash and skimming down the other side like a dragon-fly. This is the best dry Martini I've had for years.

CHARLES. Will you have another?

MADAME ARCATI (*holding out her glass*) Certainly.

(CHARLES *takes her glass and refills it at the drinks table*)

You're a very clever man. Anybody can write books, but it takes an artist to make a dry Martini that's dry enough.

RUTH. Are you writing anything nowadays, Madame Arcati?

MADAME ARCATI. Every morning regular as clockwork, seven till one.

CHARLES (*giving* MADAME ARCATI *a cocktail*) Is it a novel or a memoir?

MADAME ARCATI. It's a children's book. I have to finish it by the end of October to catch the Christmas sales. It's mostly about very small animals; the hero is a moss beetle.

(MRS BRADMAN *laughs nervously*)

I had to give up my memoir of Princess Palliatani because she died in April. I talked to her about it the other day and she implored me to go on with it. But I really hadn't the heart.

MRS BRADMAN (*incredulously*) You *talked* to her about it the other day?

MADAME ARCATI. Yes, through my control, of course. She sounded very irritable.

MRS BRADMAN. It's funny to think of people in the spirit world being irritable, isn't it? I mean, one can hardly imagine it, can one?

CHARLES (*coming down on the left of Ruth*) We have no reliable guarantee that the after life will be any less exasperating than this one, have we?

MRS BRADMAN (*laughing*) Oh, Mr Condomine, how *can* you?

RUTH. I expect it's dreadfully ignorant of me not to know—but who was Princess Palliatani?

MADAME ARCATI. She was originally a Jewess from Odessa of quite remarkable beauty. It was an accepted fact that people used to stand on the seats of railway stations to watch her whizz by.

CHARLES. She was a keen traveller?

MADAME ARCATI. In her younger days, yes. Later on she married a Mr Clarke in the Consular Service and settled down for a while.

RUTH. How did she become Princess Palliatani?

MADAME ARCATI. That was years later. Mr Clarke passed over and left her penniless with two strapping girls.

RUTH. How unpleasant.

MADAME ARCATI. And so there was nothing for it but to obey

the beckoning finger of adventure and take to the road again. So off she went, bag and baggage, to Vladivostock.

CHARLES. What an extraordinary place to go!

MADAME ARCATI. She had cousins there. Some years later she met old Palliatani, who was returning from a secret mission in Japan. He was immediately staggered by her beauty and very shortly afterwards married her. From then on her life became really interesting.

DR BRADMAN. I should hardly have described it as dull before.

RUTH. What happened to the girls?

MADAME ARCATI. She neither saw them nor spoke to them for twenty-three years.

MRS BRADMAN. How extraordinary.

MADAME ARCATI. Not at all. She was always very erratic emotionally.

(*The door of the dining-room opens and* EDITH *comes in*)

EDITH (*nervously*) Dinner is served, mum.

RUTH. Thank you, Edith. Shall we——?

(EDITH *retires backwards into the dining-room. They all rise*)

MADAME ARCATI. No red meat, I hope?

RUTH. There's meat, but I don't think it will be very red. Would you rather have an egg or something?

MADAME ARCATI. No, thank you. It's just that I make it a rule never to eat red meat before I work. It sometimes has an odd effect . . .

CHARLES. What sort of effect?

MADAME ARCATI. Oh, nothing of the least importance. If it isn't very red, it won't matter much. Anyhow, we'll risk it.

(MADAME ARCATI *goes out first with* RUTH, *followed by* MRS BRADMAN, DR BRADMAN *and* CHARLES)

RUTH. Come along, then. Mrs Bradman—Madame Arcati—you're on Charles's right. . . .

(*They all move into the dining-room as the lights fade on the scene*)

(*Light Cue No. 2. Act I, Scene 1*)

CURTAIN

SCENE 2

(*Light Cue No. 1. Act I, Scene 2*)

When the LIGHTS *go up, dinner is over, and* RUTH, MRS BRADMAN *and* MADAME ARCATI *are sitting having their coffee;* MRS BRADMAN *on the pouffe down stage* R. MADAME ARCATI *on the* R *end of the sofa,*

RUTH *on the* L *end of the sofa. All have coffee-cups. The doors are open, the windows are closed and the curtains are half closed.*

MADAME ARCATI. . . . on her mother's side she went right back to the Borgias, which I think accounted for a lot one way or another. Even as a child she was given to the most violent destructive tempers. Very inbred, you know.

MRS BRADMAN. Yes; she must have been.

MADAME ARCATI. My control was quite scared the other day when we were talking. I could hear it in her voice. After all, she's only a child.

RUTH. Do you always have a child as a control?

MADAME ARCATI. Yes, they're generally the best. Some mediums prefer Indians, of course, but personally I've always found them unreliable.

RUTH. In what way unreliable?

MADAME ARCATI. Well, for one thing, they're frightfully lazy, and also, when faced with any sort of difficulty, they're rather apt to go off into their own tribal language, which is naturally unintelligible. That generally spoils everything and wastes a great deal of time. No, children are undoubtedly more satisfactory, particularly when they get to know you and understand your ways. Daphne has worked with me for years.

MRS BRADMAN. And she still goes on being a child? I mean, she doesn't show signs of growing any older?

MADAME ARCATI (*patiently*) Time values on the Other Side are utterly different from ours.

MRS BRADMAN. Do you feel funny when you go off into a trance?

MADAME ARCATI. In what way funny?

RUTH (*hastily*) Mrs Bradman doesn't mean funny in its comic implication; I think she meant odd or strange.

MADAME ARCATI. The word was an unfortunate choice.

MRS BRADMAN. I'm sure I'm very sorry.

MADAME ARCATI. It doesn't matter in the least. Please don't apologize.

RUTH. When did you first discover that you had these extraordinary powers?

MADAME ARCATI. When I was quite tiny. My mother was a medium before me, you know, and so I had every opportunity of starting on the ground floor, as you might say. I had my first trance when I was four years old and my first ectoplasmic manifestation when I was five and a half. What an exciting day that was! I shall never forget it. Of course the manifestation itself was quite small and of very short duration, but, for a child of my tender years, it was most gratifying.

MRS BRADMAN. Your mother must have been so pleased.

MADAME ARCATI (*modestly*) She was.

MRS BRADMAN. Can you foretell the future?

MADAME ARCATI. Certainly not. I disapprove of fortune tellers most strongly.

MRS BRADMAN (*disappointed*) Oh, really? Why?

MADAME ARCATI. Too much guesswork and fake mixed up with it, even when the gift is genuine. And it only very occasionally is. You can't count on it.

RUTH. Why not?

MADAME ARCATI. Time again. Time is the reef upon which all our frail mystic ships are wrecked.

RUTH. You mean because it has never yet been proved that the past and the present and the future are not one and the same thing.

MADAME ARCATI. I long ago came to the conclusion that nothing has ever been definitely proved about anything.

RUTH. How very wise.

(MADAME ARCATI *hands her cup to* RUTH. MRS BRADMAN *puts her cup behind her on the small table down stage* R. EDITH *comes in with a tray of drinks. She puts the tray down on the* C *table by Ruth.* RUTH *moves a coffee-cup and a vase to make room for it. She takes the cigarette-box and the ash tray from the table and gives them to* EDITH, *who puts them on the drinks table*)

I want you to leave the dining-room just as it is for tonight, Edith. You can clear the table in the morning.

EDITH. Yes'm.

RUTH. And we don't want to be disturbed for the next hour or so for any reason whatsoever. Is that clear?

EDITH. Yes'm.

RUTH. And if anyone should telephone, just say we are out and take a message.

MRS BRADMAN. Unless it's an urgent call for George.

RUTH. Unless it's an urgent call for Doctor Bradman.

EDITH. Yes'm.

(EDITH *goes out swiftly*)

RUTH. There's not likely to be one, is there?

MRS BRADMAN. No, I don't think so.

MADAME ARCATI. Once I am off it won't matter, but an interruption during the preliminary stages might be disastrous.

MRS BRADMAN. I wish the men would hurry up. I'm terribly excited.

MADAME ARCATI. Please don't be. It makes everything much, much more difficult.

(CHARLES *and* DR BRADMAN *come out of the dining-room. They are smoking cigars.* DR BRADMAN *comes to the fireplace and* CHARLES *to the* L *arm of the armchair*)

CHARLES (*cheerfully*) Well, Madame Arcati—the time is drawing near.

MADAME ARCATI. Who knows? It may be receding!

CHARLES. How very true.

DR BRADMAN. I hope you feel in the mood, Madame Arcati.

MADAME ARCATI. It isn't a question of mood. It's a question of concentration.

RUTH. You must forgive us being impatient. We can perfectly easily wait though, if you're not quite ready to start.

MADAME ARCATI. Nonsense, my dear, I'm absolutely ready. (*She rises*) Heigho, heigho, to work we go!

CHARLES. Is there anything you'd like us to do?

MADAME ARCATI. Do?

CHARLES. Yes—hold hands or anything?

MADAME ARCATI. All that will come later. (*She goes to the window*)

(*The others all rise*)

First a few deep, deep breaths of fresh air—— (*Over her shoulder*) You may talk if you wish, it will not disturb me in the least. (*She flings the windows wide open and inhales deeply and a trifle noisily*)

RUTH (*with a quizzical glance at Charles*) Oh dear!

CHARLES (*putting his finger to his lips warningly*) An excellent dinner, darling. I congratulate you.

RUTH. The mousse wasn't quite right.

CHARLES. It looked a bit hysterical, but it tasted delicious.

MADAME ARCATI. That cuckoo is very angry.

CHARLES. I beg your pardon?

MADAME ARCATI. I said that cuckoo is very angry. Listen.

(*They all listen obediently*)

CHARLES. How can you tell?

MADAME ARCATI. Timbre. No moon; that's as well, I think. There's mist rising from the marshes. (*A thought strikes her*) There's no need for me to light my bicycle lamp, is there? I mean, nobody is likely to fall over it?

RUTH. No, we're not expecting anybody else.

MADAME ARCATI. Good night, you foolish bird. (*She closes the windows*) You have a table?

CHARLES. Yes. We thought that one would do.

MADAME ARCATI (*putting her hands on the small table below the piano and then pointing to the* C *table*) I think the one that has the drinks on it would be better.

(DR BRADMAN *comes to the* C *table and takes the tray from it and puts it up stage* R *on the drinks table, closes the doors and brings the chair from* R *of the door to down stage* L. CHARLES *brings the* C *table over to* L *between the armchair and the gramophone*)

Dr Bradman. Change over.

Charles (to Ruth) You told Edith we didn't want to be disturbed?

Ruth. Yes, darling.

Madame Arcati (crossing below the séance table, over to the mantelpiece. Then she walks about the room—twisting and untwisting her hands) This is a moment I always hate.

Ruth. Are you nervous?

Madame Arcati. Yes. When I was a girl I always used to be sick.

Dr Bradman. How fortunate that you grew out of it.

(Ruth gets the desk-chair from up stage r and brings it to lc above the table)

Ruth (hurriedly) Children are always much more prone to be sick than grown-ups, though, aren't they? I know I could never travel in a train with any degree of safety until I was fourteen.

(Madame Arcati is now walking rc above the sofa. Mrs Bradman brings the pouffe over to r of the séance table)

Madame Arcati (still walking) 'Little Tommy Tucker sings for his supper. What shall he have but brown bread and butter?' I despise that because it doesn't rhyme at all; but Daphne loves it.

(Madame Arcati has now arrived below the sofa. The others are grouped round the séance table, Dr Bradman down l, Ruth on his r, then Charles and Mrs Bradman by the pouffe)

Dr Bradman. Who's Daphne?

Ruth. Daphne is Madame Arcati's control. She's a little girl.

Dr Bradman. Oh, I see—yes, of course.

Charles. How old is she?

Madame Arcati. Rising seven when she died.

Mrs Bradman. And when was that?

Madame Arcati. February the sixth, eighteen eighty-four.

Mrs Bradman. Poor little thing.

(Dr Bradman brings the chair above the gramophone to the table)

Dr Bradman. She must be a bit long in the tooth by now, I should think.

Madame Arcati (at the fireplace. She stops walking and addresses Dr Bradman across the stage) You should think, Doctor Bradman, but I fear you don't; at least, not profoundly enough.

Mrs Bradman. Do be quiet, George. You'll put Madame Arcati off.

Madame Arcati. Don't worry, my dear, I am quite used to sceptics. They generally turn out to be the most vulnerable and receptive in the long run.

RUTH. You'd better take that warning to heart, Doctor Bradman.

DR BRADMAN. Please forgive me, Madame Arcati. I can assure you I am most deeply interested.

MADAME ARCATI. It is of no consequence. Will you all sit round the table, please, and place your hands downwards on it?

RUTH. Come, Mrs Bradman——

CHARLES. What about the lights?

MADAME ARCATI. All in good time, Mr Condomine. Sit down, please.

(*The four of them sit down at each side of the séance table.* RUTH *is up stage facing* MRS BRADMAN. CHARLES *on Ruth's* R. DR BRADMAN *on Ruth's* L. MADAME ARCATI *comes to above the table between Ruth and Dr Bradman and surveys them critically, her head on one side. She is whistling a little tune. Then she sings*)

The fingers should be touching . . . that's right. I presume that that is the gramophone, Mr Condomine?

CHARLES (*half rising*) Yes. Would you like me to start it? It's an electric one.

MADAME ARCATI. Please stay where you are. I can manage. (*She moves to the gramophone* L *and picks up the record album from the rack below it*) Now let me see—what have we here? Brahms—oh dear me, no; Rachmaninoff—too florid. Where is the dance music?

RUTH. They're the loose ones on the left.

MADAME ARCATI. I see. (*She stoops down and produces a pile of dance records*)

CHARLES. I'm afraid they're none of them very new.

MADAME ARCATI. Daphne is really more attached to Irving Berlin than anybody else. She likes a tune she can hum. Ah, here's one—'Always'.

CHARLES (*half jumping up again*) 'Always'!

RUTH. Do sit down, Charles. What *is* the matter?

CHARLES (*subsiding*) Nothing—nothing at all.

MADAME ARCATI. The light switch is by the door?

RUTH. Yes, all except the small one on the desk, and the gramophone.

MADAME ARCATI (*moving above them to* C *on* R *of Ruth*) Very well, I understand.

RUTH. Charles, do keep still.

MRS BRADMAN. Fingers touching, George. Remember what Madame Arcati said.

MADAME ARCATI. Now there are one or two things that I should like to explain; so will you all listen attentively?

RUTH. Of course.

MADAME ARCATI. Presently, when the music begins, I am going to switch out the lights. I may then either walk about the

room for a little or lie down flat. In due course I shall draw up
this dear little stool and join you at the table. I shall place myself
between you and your wife, Mr Condomine, and rest my hands
lightly upon yours. I must ask you not to address me or move or
do anything in the least distracting. Is that quite, quite clear?

CHARLES. Perfectly.

MADAME ARCATI. Of course, I cannot guarantee that anything
will happen at all. Daphne may be unavailable. She had a head
cold very recently, and was rather under the weather, poor child.
On the other hand, a great many things might occur. One of you
might have an emanation, for instance; or we might contact a
poltergeist, which would be extremely destructive and noisy.

RUTH (anxiously) In what way destructive?

MADAME ARCATI. They throw things, you know.

RUTH. No, I didn't know.

MADAME ARCATI. But we must cross that bridge when we come
to it, mustn't we?

CHARLES. Certainly—by all means.

MADAME ARCATI. Fortunately an Elemental at this time of the
year is most unlikely.

RUTH. What do Elementals do?

MADAME ARCATI. Oh, my dear, one can never tell. They're
dreadfully unpredictable. Usually they take the form of a very
cold wind.

MRS BRADMAN. I don't think I shall like that.

MADAME ARCATI. Occasionally reaching almost hurricane
velocity.

RUTH. You don't think it would be a good idea to take the
more breakable ornaments off the mantelpiece before we start?

MADAME ARCATI (indulgently) That really is not necessary, Mrs
Condomine. I assure you I have my own methods of dealing with
Elementals.

RUTH. I'm so glad.

MADAME ARCATI. Now, then; are you ready to empty your
minds?

DR BRADMAN. Do you mean we're to try to think of nothing?

MADAME ARCATI. Absolutely nothing, Doctor Bradman. Concentrate on a space or a nondescript colour. That's really the best
way.

DR BRADMAN. I'll do my damnedest.

MADAME ARCATI. Good work!—I will now start the music.

(*She goes to the gramophone, puts on the record of 'Always', and
begins to walk about the room; occasionally she moves into an abortive
little dance step. Then with sudden speed, she runs across the room and
switches off the lights*)

Lights!

(*Light Cue No. 2. Act I, Scene 2*)

Mrs Bradman. Oh dear!

Madame Arcati. Quiet—please!

(*In the gloom* Madame Arcati, *after wandering about a little, brings the stool from under the piano to between Ruth and Charles and sits at the table. The gramophone record comes to an end. There is dead silence*)

Is there anyone there? ... (*A long pause*) ... Is there anyone there? ... (*Another long pause*) ... One rap for yes ... two raps for no. Now then ... is there anyone there?

(*After a shorter pause, the table gives a little bump*)

Mrs Bradman (*involuntarily*) Oh!

Madame Arcati. Sshhh! ... Is that you, Daphne? (*The table gives a louder bump*) Is your cold better, dear? (*The table gives two loud bumps, very quickly*) Oh, I'm so sorry. Are you doing anything for it? (*The table bumps several times*) I'm afraid she's rather fretful ... (*There is a silence*) Is there anyone there who wishes to speak to anyone here? (*After a pause the table gives one bump*) Ah! Now we're getting somewhere ... No, Daphne, don't do that, dear, you're hurting me ... Daphne, dear, please ... Oh, oh, oh! ... be good, there's a dear child ... You say there is someone there who wishes to speak to someone here? (*One bump*) Is it me? (*Two sharp bumps*) Is it Doctor Bradman? (*Two bumps*) Is it Mrs Bradman? (*Two bumps*) Is it Mrs Condomine? (*Several very loud bumps, which continue until* Madame Arcati *shouts it down*) Stop it! Behave yourself! Is it Mr Condomine? (*There is dead silence for a moment, and then a very loud single bump*) There's someone who wishes to speak to you, Mr Condomine.

Charles. Tell them to leave a message.

(*The table bangs about loudly*)

Madame Arcati. I really must ask you not to be flippant, Mr Condomine.

Ruth. Charles, how can you be so idiotic? You'll spoil everything.

Charles. I'm sorry; it slipped out.

Madame Arcati. Do you know anybody who has passed over recently?

Charles. Not recently, except my cousin in the Civil Service, and he wouldn't be likely to want to communicate with me. We haven't spoken for years.

Madame Arcati (*hysterically*) Are you Mr Condomine's cousin in the Civil Service? (*The table bumps violently several times*) I'm afraid we've drawn a blank. Can't you think of anyone else? Rack your brains.

Ruth (*helpfully*) It might be old Mrs Plummett, you know. She died on Whit-Monday.

CHARLES. I can't imagine why old Mrs Plummett should wish to talk to me. We had very little in common.

RUTH. It's worth trying, anyhow.

MADAME ARCATI. Are you old Mrs Plummett?

(*The table remains still*)

RUTH. She was very deaf. Perhaps you'd better shout.

MADAME ARCATI (*shouting*) Are you old Mrs Plummett? (*Nothing happens*) There's nobody there at all.

MRS BRADMAN. How disappointing; just as we were getting on so nicely.

DR BRADMAN. Violet, be quiet.

MADAME ARCATI (*rising*) Well, I'm afraid there's nothing for it but for me to go into a trance. I had hoped to avoid it because it's so exhausting—however, what must be must be. Excuse me a moment while I start the gramophone again. (*She comes to the gramophone*)

CHARLES (*in a strained voice*) Not 'Always'. Don't play 'Always'——

RUTH. Why ever not, Charles? Don't be absurd.

MADAME ARCATI (*gently*) I'm afraid I must. It would be imprudent to change horses in midstream, if you know what I mean. (*She restarts the gramophone*)

CHARLES. Have it your own way.

(MADAME ARCATI *starts to moan and comes back slowly to the stool and sits. Then in the darkness a child's voice is heard reciting rather breathlessly:* 'Little Tommy Tucker')

DR BRADMAN. That would be Daphne. She ought to have had her adenoids out.

MRS BRADMAN. George—please.

(MADAME ARCATI *suddenly gives a loud scream and falls off the stool on to the floor*)

CHARLES. Good God!

RUTH. Keep still, Charles . . .

(CHARLES *subsides. Everyone sits in silence for a moment, then the table starts bouncing about*)

MRS BRADMAN. It's trying to get away. I can't hold it.

RUTH. Press down hard.

(*The table falls over with a crash*)

There now!

MRS BRADMAN. Ought we to pick it up or leave it where it is?

DR BRADMAN. How the hell do I know?

MRS BRADMAN. There's no need to snap at me.

ELVIRA (*behind the fireplace opening, on the other side, a perfectly strange and very charming voice*) Leave it where it is.

CHARLES. Who said that?

RUTH. Who said what?

CHARLES. Somebody said 'Leave it where it is.'

RUTH. Nonsense, dear.

CHARLES. I heard it distinctly.

RUTH. Well, nobody else did—did they?

MRS BRADMAN. I never heard a sound.

CHARLES. It was you, Ruth. You're playing tricks.

RUTH. I'm not doing anything of the sort. I haven't uttered.

(*There is another pause, and then the voice says:*)

ELVIRA (*behind the doorway* C) Good evening, Charles.

CHARLES (*very agitated*) Ventriloquism—that's what it is—ventriloquism.

RUTH (*irritably*) What is the matter with you?

CHARLES. You must have heard that. One of you must have heard that!

RUTH. Heard *what*?

CHARLES. You mean to sit there solemnly and tell me that you none of you heard anything at all?

DR BRADMAN. I certainly didn't.

MRS BRADMAN. Neither did I. I wish I had. I should love to hear something.

RUTH. It's you who are playing the tricks, Charles. You're acting to try to frighten us.

CHARLES (*breathlessly*) I'm not. I swear I'm not.

ELVIRA (*behind the windows*) It's difficult to think of what to say after seven years, but I suppose good evening is as good as anything else.

CHARLES (*intensely*) Who are you?

ELVIRA (*as before*) Elvira, of course—don't be so silly.

CHARLES. I can't bear this for another minute . . . (*He rises violently*) Get up, everybody—the entertainment's over.

(*Light Cue No. 3. Act I, Scene 2*)

(*He rushes across the room and switches on the lights. Then he moves to the fireplace. All the others rise. MADAME ARCATI is on the floor, her head towards the audience and her feet on the stool*)

RUTH. Oh, Charles, how tiresome of you. Just as we were beginning to enjoy ourselves.

CHARLES. Never again—that's all I can say. Never, never again as long as I live.

RUTH. What on earth's the matter with you?

CHARLES. Nothing's the matter with me. I'm just sick of the whole business, that's all.

DR BRADMAN. Did you hear anything that we didn't hear really?

CHARLES (*with a forced laugh*) Of course not—I was only pretending.

RUTH. I know you were.

MRS BRADMAN. Oh dear—look at Madame Arcati!

(MADAME ARCATI *is still lying on the floor with her feet upon the stool from which she fell. She is obviously quite unconscious*)

RUTH. What are we to do with her?

CHARLES. Bring her round—bring her round as soon as possible.

DR BRADMAN (*going over and kneeling down beside her*) I think we'd better leave her alone.

RUTH. But she might stay like that for hours.

(DR BRADMAN *is kneeling* L *of Madame Arcati,* RUTH *is above her.* MRS BRADMAN *to the* L *of Dr Bradman.* CHARLES *goes to the* R *of Madame Arcati below the sofa*)

DR BRADMAN (*after feeling her pulse and examining her eye*) She's out all right.

CHARLES (*almost hysterically*) Bring her round! It's dangerous to leave her like that.

RUTH. Really, Charles, you are behaving most peculiarly.

CHARLES (*kneeling* R *of* MADAME ARCATI, *shaking her violently*) Wake up, Madame Arcati! Wake up! It's time to go home!

DR BRADMAN. Here—go easy, old man!

CHARLES. Get some brandy—give her some brandy, lift her into the chair—help me, Bradman!

(RUTH *goes to the drinks table* L *and pours out some brandy.* CHARLES *and* DR BRADMAN *lift* MADAME ARCATI *and put her in the armchair.* MRS BRADMAN *takes the stool from her feet and puts it back under the piano*)

(*Leaning over her*) Wake up, Madame Arcati! Little Tommy Tucker, Madame Arcati!

(RUTH *brings the brandy to above the armchair.* CHARLES *takes it and gives some to* MADAME ARCATI *on her* R. DR BRADMAN *pats her hand on her* L. MRS BRADMAN *is above Dr Bradman*)

RUTH. Here's the brandy.

(MADAME ARCATI *gives a slight moan and a shiver*)

CHARLES (*forcing some brandy between her lips*) Wake up!

(MADAME ARCATI *gives a prolonged shiver and chokes slightly over the brandy*)

MRS BRADMAN. She's coming round.

RUTH. Be careful, Charles, you're spilling it all down her dress.

MADAME ARCATI (*opening her eyes*) Well, that's that.

RUTH (*solicitously*) Are you all right?

MADAME ARCATI. Certainly I am. Never felt better in my life.

CHARLES. Would you like some more brandy?

MADAME ARCATI. So that's the funny taste in my mouth. Well, really! Fancy allowing them to give me brandy, Doctor Bradman. You ought to have known better—brandy on top of a trance might have been catastrophic. Take it away, please. I probably shan't sleep a wink tonight as it is.

CHARLES. I know I shan't.

RUTH. Why on earth not?

(CHARLES *moves away to* R *to the fireplace and takes a cigarette*)

CHARLES. The whole experience has unhinged me.

MADAME ARCATI. Well, what happened? Was it satisfactory?

RUTH. Nothing much happened, Madame Arcati, after you went off.

MADAME ARCATI. Something happened all right, I can feel it—— (*She rises, crosses to the fireplace, above Charles, and sniffs*) No poltergeist, at any rate—that's a good thing. Any apparitions?

DR BRADMAN. Not a thing.

MADAME ARCATI. No ectoplasm?

RUTH. I'm not quite sure what it is, but I don't think so.

MADAME ARCATI. Very curious. I feel as though something tremendous has taken place.

RUTH. Charles pretended he heard a voice in order to frighten us.

CHARLES (*lighting a cigarette*) It was only a joke.

MADAME ARCATI. A very poor one, if I may say so (*She goes round above the sofa to* RC) Nevertheless, I am prepared to swear that there is someone else psychic in this room apart from myself.

RUTH. I don't see how there can be really, Madame Arcati.

MADAME ARCATI. I do hope I haven't gone and released something. However, we are bound to find out within a day or two. If any manifestation should occur or you hear any unexpected noises, you might let me know at once.

RUTH. Of course we will. We'll telephone immediately.

MADAME ARCATI. I think I really must be on my way now.

RUTH. Wouldn't you like anything before you go?

MADAME ARCATI. No, thank you. I have some Ovaltine all ready in a saucepan at home; it only needs hotting up.

DR BRADMAN. Wouldn't you like to leave your bicycle here and let us drive you?

MRS BRADMAN. I honestly do think you should, Madame Arcati. After that trance and everything you can't be feeling quite yourself.

MADAME ARCATI. Nonsense, my dear, I'm as fit as a fiddle.

Always feel capital after a trance—rejuvenates me. Good night, Mrs Condomine.

RUTH. It was awfully sweet of you to take so much trouble.

MADAME ARCATI. I'm so sorry so little occurred. It's that cold of Daphne's, I expect. You know what children are when they have anything wrong with them. We must try again some other evening.

(MADAME ARCATI *crosses above Ruth to* R *of Mrs Bradman*)

RUTH. That would be lovely.

MADAME ARCATI (*shaking hands with* MRS BRADMAN) Good night, Mrs Bradman.

MRS BRADMAN. It was thrilling, it really was. I felt the table absolutely shaking under my hands.

(MADAME ARCATI *crosses to* DR BRADMAN *and shakes hands*)

MADAME ARCATI. Good night, Doctor.

DR BRADMAN. Congratulations, Madame Arcati.

MADAME ARCATI. I am fully aware of the irony in your voice, Doctor Bradman. As a matter of fact you'd be an admirable subject for telepathic hypnosis. A great chum of mine is an expert. I should like her to look you over.

DR BRADMAN. I'm sure I should be charmed.

MADAME ARCATI. Good night, everyone. Next time we must really put our backs into it!

(*With a comprehensive smile and a wave of the hand, she goes out, followed by* CHARLES.

RUTH *sinks down into the sofa, laughing helplessly.* MRS BRADMAN *comes and sits* L *of the armchair.* DR BRADMAN *picks up the séance table and puts the desk-chair back up stage* R, *then comes back and puts the pouffe back in position down stage* R. *He then returns to* LC)

RUTH. Oh dear! . . . oh dear!

MRS BRADMAN (*beginning to laugh too*) Be careful, Mrs Condomine; she might hear you.

RUTH. I can't help it. I really can't. I've been holding this in for ages.

MRS BRADMAN. She certainly put you in your place, George, and serve you right.

RUTH. She's raving mad, of course; mad as a hatter.

MRS BRADMAN. But do you really think she *believes*?

DR BRADMAN. Of course not. The whole thing's a put-up job. I must say, though, she shoots a more original line than they generally do.

RUTH. I should think that she's probably half convinced herself by now.

DR BRADMAN. Possibly. The trance was genuine enough; but that, of course, is easily accounted for.

RUTH. Hysteria?

DR BRADMAN. Yes—a form of hysteria, I should imagine.

MRS BRADMAN. I do hope Mr Condomine got all the atmosphere he wanted for his book.

RUTH. He might have got a great deal more if he hadn't spoiled everything by showing off . . . I'm really very cross with him.

(Light Cue No. 4. Act I, Scene 2)

(At this moment ELVIRA comes in through the french windows. She is charmingly dressed in a sort of négligée. Everything about her is grey; hair, skin, dress, hands, so we must accept the fact that she is not quite of this world. She passes between DR and MRS BRADMAN and RUTH while they are talking. None of them sees her. She moves to the fireplace, then comes round the sofa to below the piano, where she leans. She regards them with interest, a slight smile on her face)

I suddenly felt a draught—there must be a window open.

DR BRADMAN *(looking)* No—they're shut.

MRS BRADMAN *(laughing)* Perhaps it was one of those what you may call 'ems that Madame Arcati was talking about.

DR BRADMAN. Elementals.

RUTH *(also laughing again)* Oh no, it couldn't be. She distinctly said that it was the wrong time of the year for Elementals.

(CHARLES comes in and moves to the armchair C)

CHARLES. Well, the old girl's gone pedalling off down the drive at the hell of a speed. We had a bit of trouble lighting her lamp.

MRS BRADMAN. Poor thing.

CHARLES. I've got a theory about her, you know. I believe she is completely sincere.

RUTH. Charles! How could she be?

CHARLES. Wouldn't it be possible, Doctor? Some form of self-hypnotism?

DR BRADMAN. It might be. As I was explaining to your wife just now, there are certain types of hysterical subjects . . .

MRS BRADMAN. George, dear, it's getting terribly late, we really must go home. You have to get up so early in the morning.

DR BRADMAN. You see? The moment I begin to talk about anything that really interests me, my wife interrupts me.

MRS BRADMAN. You know I'm right, darling—it's past eleven.

DR BRADMAN *(moves to Charles C)* I'll do a little reading up on the whole business; just for the fun of it.

CHARLES. You must have a drink before you go.

DR BRADMAN. No, really, thank you. Violet's quite right, I'm afraid. I have got to get up abominably early tomorrow. I have a patient being operated on in Canterbury.

(MRS BRADMAN goes to Ruth, below the sofa. RUTH rises)

MRS BRADMAN. It has been a thrilling evening. I shall never forget it. It was sweet of you to include us.

DR BRADMAN. Good night, Mrs Condomine. Thank you so much.

CHARLES. You're sure about the drink?

DR BRADMAN. Quite sure, thanks.

RUTH. We'll let you know if we find any poltergeists whirling about.

DR BRADMAN. I should never forgive you if you didn't.

MRS BRADMAN. Come along, darling.

(*The* BRADMANS *exeunt, followed by* CHARLES.

RUTH *crosses to the piano, leans over Elvira and gets a cigarette and lights it, then crosses back to the fireplace as* CHARLES *comes back into the room*)

RUTH. Well, darling?

CHARLES (L *end of the sofa. Absently*) Well?

RUTH. Would you say the evening had been profitable?

CHARLES. Yes—I suppose so.

RUTH. I must say it was extremely funny at moments.

CHARLES. Yes—it certainly was.

RUTH. What's the matter?

CHARLES. The matter?

RUTH. Yes. You seem old, somehow. Do you feel quite well?

CHARLES. Perfectly. I think I'll have a drink. Do you want one?

RUTH. No, thank you, dear.

CHARLES (*moving to the drinks table and pouring out a whisky and soda*) It's rather chilly in this room.

RUTH. Come over by the fire.

CHARLES. I don't think I'll make any notes tonight. I'll start fresh in the morning.

(CHARLES *turns, the glass in his hand. He sees Elvira and drops the glass on the floor*)

My God!

RUTH. Charles!

ELVIRA. That was very clumsy, Charles dear.

CHARLES. Elvira!—then it's true—it was you!

ELVIRA. Of course it was.

RUTH (*starts to go to Charles*) Charles—darling Charles—what are you talking about?

CHARLES (*to Elvira*) Are you a ghost?

ELVIRA (*crossing below the sofa to the fire*) I suppose I must be. It's all very confusing.

RUTH (*moving to* R *of Charles and becoming agitated*) Charles—what do you keep looking over there for? Look at me. What's happened?

CHARLES. Don't you see?

RUTH. See what?

CHARLES. Elvira.

RUTH (*staring at him incredulously*) Elvira!!

CHARLES (*with an effort at social grace*) Yes. Elvira dear, this is Ruth. Ruth, this is Elvira.

(RUTH *tries to take his arm.* CHARLES *retreats down stage* L)

RUTH (*with forced calmness*) Come and sit down, darling.

CHARLES. Do you mean to say you can't see her?

RUTH. Listen, Charles—you just sit down quietly by the fire and I'll mix you another drink. Don't worry about the mess on the carpet, Edith can clean it up in the morning. (*She takes him by the arm*)

CHARLES (*breaking away*) But you must be able to see her—she's there—look—right in front of you—there!

RUTH. Are you mad! What's happened to you?

CHARLES. You can't see her?

RUTH. If this is a joke, dear, it's gone quite far enough. Sit down, for God's sake, and don't be idiotic.

CHARLES (*clutching his head*) What am I to do! What the hell am I to do!

ELVIRA. I think you might at least be a little more pleased to see me. After all, you conjured me up.

CHARLES. I didn't do any such thing.

ELVIRA. Nonsense; of course you did. That awful child with the cold came and told me you wanted to see me urgently.

CHARLES. It was all a mistake, a horrible mistake.

RUTH. Stop talking like that, Charles. As I told you before the joke's gone far enough.

CHARLES. I've gone mad, that's what it is, I've just gone raving mad.

RUTH (*pouring out some brandy and bringing it to Charles below the piano*) Here—drink this.

CHARLES (*mechanically—taking it*) This is appalling!

RUTH. Relax.

CHARLES. How can I relax? I shall never be able to relax again as long as I live.

RUTH. Drink some brandy.

CHARLES (*drinking it at a gulp*) There! Now are you satisfied?

RUTH. Now sit down.

CHARLES. Why are you so anxious for me to sit down? What good will that do?

RUTH. I want you to relax. You can't relax standing up.

ELVIRA. African natives can. They can stand on one leg for hours.

CHARLES. I don't happen to be an African native.

RUTH. You don't happen to be a *what*?

CHARLES (*savagely*) An African native!

RUTH. What's that got to do with it?

CHARLES. It doesn't matter, Ruth; really it doesn't matter.

(CHARLES *sits in the armchair.* RUTH *moves above him*)

We'll say no more about it. See, I've sat down.

RUTH. Would you like some more brandy?

CHARLES. Yes, please.

(RUTH *goes up to the drinks table with the glass*)

ELVIRA. Very unwise. You always had a weak head.

CHARLES. I could drink you under the table. .

RUTH. There's no need to be aggressive, Charles. I'm doing my best to help you.

CHARLES. I'm sorry.

RUTH (*coming to Charles with the brandy*) Here, drink this; and then we'll go to bed.

ELVIRA. Get rid of her, Charles; then we can talk in peace.

CHARLES. That's a thoroughly immoral suggestion. You ought to be ashamed of yourself.

RUTH. What is there immoral in that?

CHARLES. I wasn't talking to you.

RUTH. Who were you talking to, then?

CHARLES. Elvira, of course.

RUTH. To hell with Elvira!

ELVIRA. There now—she's getting cross.

CHARLES. I don't blame her.

RUTH. What don't you blame her for?

CHARLES (*rising and backing downstage L a pace*) Oh, God!

RUTH. Now, look here, Charles. I gather you've got some sort of plan behind all this. I'm not quite a fool. I suspected you when we were doing that idiotic séance.

CHARLES. Don't be so silly. What plan could I have?

RUTH. I don't know. It's probably something to do with the characters in your book—how they, or one of them, would react to a certain situation. I refuse to be used as a guinea-pig unless I'm warned beforehand what it's all about.

CHARLES (*moving a couple of paces towards Ruth*) Elvira is here, Ruth—she's standing a few yards away from you.

RUTH (*sarcastically*) Yes, dear, I can see her distinctly—under the piano with a zebra!

CHARLES. But Ruth——

RUTH. I am not going to stay here arguing any longer.

ELVIRA. Hurray!

CHARLES. Shut up!

RUTH (*incensed*) How dare you speak to me like that?

CHARLES. Listen, Ruth. Please listen——

RUTH. I will not listen to any more of this nonsense. I am going up to bed now; I'll leave you to turn out the lights. I shan't be asleep. I'm too upset. So you can come in and say good night to me if you feel like it.

ELVIRA. That's big of her, I must say.

CHARLES. Be quiet. You're behaving like a guttersnipe.

RUTH (icily) That is all I have to say. Good night, Charles.

(RUTH *walks swiftly out of the room without looking at him again*)

CHARLES (*following Ruth to the door*) Ruth——

ELVIRA. That was one of the most enjoyable half-hours I have ever spent.

CHARLES (*putting down his glass on the drinks table*) Oh, Elvira—how could you!

ELVIRA. Poor Ruth!

CHARLES (*staring at her*) This is obviously an hallucination, isn't it?

ELVIRA. I'm afraid I don't know the technical term for it.

CHARLES (*coming down* C) What am I to do?

ELVIRA. What Ruth suggested—relax.

CHARLES (*moving below the chair to the sofa*) Where have you come from?

ELVIRA. Do you know, it's very peculiar, but I've sort of forgotten.

CHARLES. Are you to be here indefinitely?

ELVIRA. I don't know that either.

CHARLES. Oh, my God!

ELVIRA. Why? Would you hate it so much if I was?

CHARLES. Well, you must admit it would be embarrassing?

ELVIRA. I don't see why, really. It's all a question of adjusting yourself. Anyhow, I think it's horrid of you to be so unwelcoming and disagreeable.

CHARLES. Now look here, Elvira——

ELVIRA (*near tears*) I do. I think you're mean.

CHARLES. Try to see my point, dear. I've been married to Ruth for five years, and you've been dead for seven . . .

ELVIRA. Not dead, Charles. 'Passed over.' It's considered vulgar to say 'dead' where I come from.

CHARLES. Passed over, then.

ELVIRA. At any rate, now that I'm here, the least you can do is to make a pretence of being amiable about it.

CHARLES. Of course, my dear, I'm delighted in one way.

ELVIRA. I don't believe you love me any more.

CHARLES. I shall always love the memory of you.

ELVIRA (*crossing slowly above the sofa by the armchair to downstage* L) You mustn't think me unreasonable, but I really am a little hurt. You called me back; and at great inconvenience I came—and you've been thoroughly churlish ever since I arrived.

CHARLES (*gently*) Believe me, Elvira, I most emphatically did not send for you. There's been some mistake.

ELVIRA (*irritably*) Well, somebody did—and that child said it was you. I remember I was playing backgammon with a very sweet old Oriental gentleman, I think his name was Genghiz Khan, and I'd just thrown double sixes, and then the child paged me and the next thing I knew I was in this room. Perhaps it was your subconscious . . .

CHARLES. You must find out whether you are going to stay or not, and we can make arrangements accordingly.

ELVIRA. I don't see how I can.

CHARLES. Well, try to think. Isn't there anyone that you know, that you can get in touch with over there—on the other side, or whatever it's called—who could advise you?

ELVIRA. I can't think—it seems so far away—as though I'd dreamed it . . .

CHARLES. You must know somebody else besides Genghiz Khan.

ELVIRA (*moving to the armchair*) Oh, Charles . . .

CHARLES. What is it?

ELVIRA. I want to cry, but I don't think I'm able to.

CHARLES. What do you want to cry for?

ELVIRA. It's seeing you again—and you being so irascible, like you always used to be.

CHARLES. I don't mean to be irascible, Elvira.

ELVIRA. Darling—I don't mind really—I never did.

CHARLES. Is it cold—being a ghost?

ELVIRA. No—I don't think so.

CHARLES. What happens if I touch you?

ELVIRA. I doubt if you can. Do you want to?

CHARLES (*sitting at the L end of the sofa*) Oh, Elvira . . . (*He buries his face in his hands*)

ELVIRA (*moving to the L arm of the sofa*) What is it, darling?

CHARLES. I really do feel strange, seeing you again.

ELVIRA (*moving to R below the sofa and round above it again to the L arm*) That's better.

CHARLES (*looking up*) What's better?

ELVIRA. Your voice was kinder.

CHARLES. Was I ever unkind to you when you were alive?

ELVIRA. Often.

CHARLES. Oh, how can you! I'm sure that's an exaggeration.

ELVIRA. Not at all. You were an absolute pig that time we went to Cornwall and stayed in that awful hotel. You hit me with a billiard cue.

(*Light Cue No. 5. Act I, Scene 2*)

CHARLES. Only very, very gently.

ELVIRA. I loved you very much.

CHARLES. I loved you too . . . (*He puts out his hand to her and then draws it away*) No, I can't touch you. Isn't that horrible?

ELVIRA. Perhaps it's as well if I'm going to stay for any length of time. (*She sits on the L arm of the sofa*)

CHARLES. I suppose I shall wake up eventually . . . but I feel strangely peaceful now.

(*Light Cue No. 6. Act I, Scene 2*)

ELVIRA. That's right. Put your head back

CHARLES (*doing so*) Like that?

ELVIRA (*stroking his hair*) Can you feel anything?

CHARLES. Only a very little breeze through my hair . . .

ELVIRA. Well, that's better than nothing.

CHARLES (*drowsily*) I suppose if I'm really out of my mind they'll put me in an asylum.

ELVIRA. Don't worry about that—just relax.

CHARLES (*very drowsily indeed*) Poor Ruth.

ELVIRA (*gently and sweetly*) To hell with Ruth.

By now the blackout is complete

The CURTAIN *falls*

ACT II

SCENE 1

(Light Cue No. 1. Act II, Scene 1)

It is about nine-thirty the next morning. The sun is pouring in through the open french windows; the curtains are wide open. The doors are shut.

A breakfast-table is set LC below the piano. RUTH sits L of the table, her back to the window, reading 'The Times'. CHARLES comes in and kisses her.

CHARLES. Good morning, darling.

RUTH (*with a certain stiffness*) Good morning, Charles.

CHARLES (*going to the open window and taking a deep breath*) It certainly is.

RUTH. What certainly is what?

CHARLES. A good morning. A tremendously good morning! There isn't a cloud in the sky and everything looks newly washed.

RUTH (*turning a page of 'The Times'*) Edith's keeping your breakfast hot. You'd better ring.

CHARLES (*crossing to the mantelpiece and ringing the bell up stage*) Anything interesting in *The Times*?

RUTH. Don't be silly, Charles.

CHARLES. I intend to work all day.

RUTH. Good.

CHARLES (*coming back to the breakfast-table*) It's extraordinary about daylight, isn't it?

RUTH. How do you mean?

CHARLES. The way it reduces everything to normal.

RUTH. Does it?

CHARLES (*sitting R of the table opposite Ruth. Firmly*) Yes—it does.

RUTH. I'm sure I'm very glad to hear it.

CHARLES. You're very glacial this morning.

RUTH. Are you surprised?

CHARLES. Frankly, yes. I expected more of you.

RUTH. Well, really!

CHARLES. I've always looked upon you as a woman of perception and understanding.

RUTH. Perhaps this is one of my off days.

(EDITH *comes in with some bacon and eggs and toast. She comes to above the table between Charles and Ruth*)

CHARLES (*cheerfully*) Good morning, Edith.

EDITH. Good morning, sir.

CHARLES. Feeling fit?

EDITH. Yes, sir, thank you, sir.

CHARLES. How's Cook?

EDITH. I don't know, sir, I haven't asked her.

CHARLES. You should. You should begin every day by asking everyone how they are. It oils the wheels.

EDITH. Yes, sir.

CHARLES. Greet her from me, will you?

EDITH. Yes, sir.

RUTH. That will be all for the moment, Edith.

EDITH. Yes'm.

(EDITH *goes out*)

RUTH. I wish you wouldn't be facetious with the servants, Charles. It confuses them and undermines their morale.

CHARLES. I consider that point of view retrogressive, if not downright feudal.

RUTH. I don't care what you consider it. I have to run the house and you don't.

CHARLES. Are you implying that I couldn't?

RUTH. You're at liberty to try.

CHARLES. I take back what I said about it being a good morning. It's a horrid morning.

RUTH. You'd better eat your breakfast while it's hot.

CHARLES. It isn't.

RUTH (*putting down 'The Times'*) Now look here, Charles, in your younger days this display of roguish flippancy might have been alluring. In a middle-aged novelist it's nauseating.

CHARLES. Would you like me to writhe at your feet in a frenzy of self-abasement?

RUTH. That would be equally nauseating, but certainly more appropriate.

CHARLES. I really don't see what I've done that's so awful.

RUTH. You behaved abominably last night. You wounded me and insulted me.

CHARLES. I was the victim of an aberration.

RUTH. Nonsense. You were drunk.

CHARLES. Drunk?

RUTH. You had four strong Dry Martinis before dinner, a great deal too much Burgundy at dinner, Heaven knows how much Port and Kummel with Doctor Bradman while I was doing my best to entertain that mad woman—and then two double brandies later. I gave them to you myself. Of course you were drunk.

CHARLES. So that's your story, is it?

RUTH. You refused to come to bed, and finally when I came down at three in the morning to see what had happened to you, I found you in an alcoholic coma on the sofa with the fire out and your hair all over your face.

CHARLES. I was not in the least drunk, Ruth. Something happened to me last night; something very peculiar happened to me.

RUTH. Nonsense.

CHARLES. It isn't nonsense. I know it looks like nonsense now in the clear remorseless light of day, but last night it was far from being nonsense. I honestly had some sort of hallucination.

RUTH. I would really rather not discuss it any further.

CHARLES. But you must discuss it. It's very disturbing.

RUTH. There I agree with you. It showed you up in a most unpleasant light. I find that extremely disturbing.

CHARLES. I swear to you that during the séance I was convinced that I heard Elvira's voice.

RUTH. Nobody else did.

CHARLES. I can't help that. I did.

RUTH. You couldn't have.

CHARLES. And later on I was equally convinced that she was in this room. I saw her distinctly and talked to her. After you'd gone up to bed we had quite a cosy little chat.

RUTH. And you seriously expect me to believe that you weren't drunk?

CHARLES. I *know* I wasn't drunk. If I'd been all that drunk I should have a dreadful hangover now, shouldn't I?

RUTH. I'm not at all sure that you haven't.

CHARLES. I haven't got a trace of a headache—my tongue's not coated—look at it. (*He puts out his tongue*)

RUTH. I've not the least desire to look at your tongue, kindly put it in again.

CHARLES (*rising, crossing to the mantelpiece and lighting a cigarette*) I know what it is. You're frightened.

RUTH. Frightened! Rubbish. What is there to be frightened of?

CHARLES. Elvira. You wouldn't have minded all that much, even if I had been drunk; it's only because it was all mixed up with Elvira.

RUTH. I seem to remember last night before dinner telling you that your views of female psychology were rather didactic. I was right. I should have added that they were puerile.

CHARLES. That was when it all began.

RUTH. When what all began?

CHARLES (*moving up to above the R end of the sofa*) We were talking too much about Elvira. It's dangerous to have somebody very strongly in your mind when you start dabbling with the occult.

RUTH. She certainly wasn't strongly in my mind.

CHARLES. She was in mine.

RUTH. Oh, she was, was she?

CHARLES (*crossing and facing Ruth at the breakfast-table*) You tried to make me say that she was more physically attractive than you, so that you could hold it over me.

RUTH. I did not. I don't give a hoot how physically attractive she was.

CHARLES. Oh yes, you do. Your whole being is devoured with jealousy. (*He moves to the armchair*)

RUTH (*rising*) This is too much!

CHARLES (*sitting in the armchair*) Women! My God, what I think of women!

RUTH. Your view of women is academic to say the least of it. Just because you've always been dominated by them, it doesn't necessarily follow that you know anything about them.

CHARLES. I've never been dominated by anyone.

RUTH (*crossing to below the R breakfast-chair*) You were hag-ridden by your mother until you were twenty-three, then you got into the clutches of that awful Mrs Whatever her name was.

CHARLES. Mrs Winthrop-Llewellyn.

RUTH (*clearing the plates on the breakfast-table and working round with her back to Charles to above the table*) I'm not interested. Then there was Elvira. She ruled you with a rod of iron.

CHARLES. Elvira never ruled anyone, she was much too elusive. That was one of her greatest charms.

RUTH. Then there was Maud Charteris.

CHARLES. My affair with Maud Charteris lasted exactly seven and a half weeks; and she cried all the time.

RUTH. The tyranny of tears! Then there was——

CHARLES. If you wish to make an inventory of my sex life, dear, I think it only fair to tell you that you've missed out several episodes. I'll consult my diary and give you the complete list after lunch.

RUTH. It's no use trying to impress me with your routine amorous exploits . . . (*She crosses upstage* C)

CHARLES. The only woman in my whole life who's ever attempted to dominate me is you. You've been at it for years.

RUTH. That is completely untrue.

CHARLES. Oh no, it isn't. You boss me and bully me and order me about. You don't even allow me to have an hallucination if I want to.

RUTH (*coming to Charles, above the sofa*) Charles, alcohol will ruin your whole life if you allow it to get hold on you, you know.

CHARLES (*rising and coming up stage above the chair to face Ruth*) Once and for all, Ruth, I would like you to understand that what happened last night was nothing whatever to do with alcohol. You've very adroitly rationalized the whole affair to your own satisfaction, but your deductions are based on complete fallacy. I am willing to grant you that it was an aberration, some sort of odd psychic delusion brought on by suggestion or hypnosis. I was stone cold sober from first to last and extremely upset into the bargain.

RUTH. *You* were upset indeed? What about me?

CHARLES. You behaved with a stolid, obtuse lack of comprehension that frankly shocked me!

RUTH. I consider that I was remarkably patient. I shall know better next time.

CHARLES. Instead of putting out a gentle comradely hand to guide me, you shouted staccato orders at me like a sergeant-major.

RUTH. You seem to forget that you gratuitously insulted me.

CHARLES. I did not.

RUTH. You called me a guttersnipe. You told me to shut up. And when I quietly suggested that we should go up to bed you said, with the most disgusting leer, that it was an immoral suggestion.

CHARLES (*exasperated*) I was talking to Elvira!

RUTH. If you were I can only say that it conjures up a fragrant picture of your first marriage.

CHARLES. My first marriage was perfectly charming and I think it's in the worst possible taste for you to sneer at it.

RUTH. I am not nearly so interested in your first marriage as you think I am. It's your second marriage that is absorbing me at the moment. It seems to me to be on the rocks.

CHARLES. Only because you persist in taking up this ridiculous attitude.

RUTH. My attitude is that of any normal woman whose husband gets drunk and hurls abuse at her.

CHARLES (*crossing to the fireplace below the sofa. Shouting*) I was not drunk!

RUTH. Be quiet. They'll hear you in the kitchen.

CHARLES. I don't care if they hear me in the Folkestone Town Hall. I was not drunk!

RUTH. Control yourself, Charles.

CHARLES. How can I control myself in the face of your idiotic damned stubbornness? It's giving me claustrophobia.

RUTH. You'd better ring up Doctor Bradman.

(EDITH *comes in with a tray to clear away the breakfast-things*)

EDITH. Can I clear, please'm?

RUTH. Yes, Edith. (*She crosses to the window*)

EDITH. Cook wants to know about lunch, mum.

(*Light Cue No. 2. Act II, Scene 1*)

RUTH (*coldly*) Will you be in to lunch, Charles?

CHARLES. Please don't worry about me. I shall be perfectly happy with a bottle of gin in my bedroom.

RUTH. Don't be silly, dear. (*To Edith*) Tell Cook we shall both be in.

EDITH. Yes'm.

RUTH (*conversationally—after a long pause*) I'm going into Hythe this morning. Is there anything you want?

CHARLES. Yes, a great deal—but I doubt if you could get it in Hythe.

RUTH. Tell Cook to put Alka-Seltzer down on my list, will you, Edith.

EDITH. Yes'm.

RUTH (*at the window—after another long pause*) It's clouding over.

CHARLES. You have a genius for understatement.

(*In silence, but breathing heavily,* EDITH *staggers out with the tray*)

RUTH (*as* EDITH *goes*) Don't worry about the table, Edith. I'll put it away.

EDITH. Yes'm.

CHARLES (*coming over to the breakfast-table to face* RUTH, *who is folding the cloth*) Please, Ruth—be reasonable.

RUTH. I'm perfectly reasonable.

CHARLES. I wasn't pretending—I really did believe that I saw Elvira, and when I heard her voice I was appalled.

RUTH. You put up with it for five years.

(RUTH *puts the chairs back up* R *and downstage* L. CHARLES *takes the table off stage during the next few lines*)

CHARLES. When I saw her I had the shock of my life. That's why I dropped the glass.

RUTH. But you *couldn't* have seen her.

CHARLES. I know I couldn't have, but I *did*.

RUTH. I'm willing to concede, then, that you imagined you did.

CHARLES. That's what I've been trying to explain to you for hours.

RUTH (*moving to* C *below the armchair*) Well then, there's obviously something wrong with you.

CHARLES (*sitting on the* L *arm of the sofa*) Exactly; there is something wrong with me. Something fundamentally wrong with me. That's why I've been imploring your sympathy and all I got was a sterile temperance lecture.

RUTH. You had been drinking, Charles. There's no denying that.

CHARLES. No more than usual.

RUTH. Well, how do you account for it, then?

CHARLES (*frantically*) I can't account for it; that's what's so awful.

RUTH (*practically*) Did you feel quite well yesterday—during the day, I mean?

CHARLES. Of course I did.

RUTH. What did you have for lunch?

CHARLES. You ought to know, you had it with me.

RUTH (*thinking*) Let me see now, there was lemon sole and that cheese thing.

CHARLES. Why should having a cheese thing for lunch make me see my deceased wife after dinner?

RUTH. You never know. It was rather rich.

CHARLES. Why didn't you see your dead husband then? You had just as much of it as I did.

RUTH. This is not getting us anywhere at all.

CHARLES. Of course it isn't; and it won't as long as you insist on ascribing supernatural phenomena to colonic irritation.

RUTH. Supernatural grandmother.

CHARLES. I admit she'd have been much less agitating.

RUTH (*standing at the back of the armchair*) Perhaps you ought to see a nerve specialist.

CHARLES. I am not in the least neurotic and never have been.

RUTH. A psycho-analyst, then.

CHARLES. I refuse to endure months of expensive humiliation only to be told at the end of it that at the age of four I was in love with my rocking-horse.

RUTH. What do you suggest, then?

CHARLES. I don't suggest anything, I'm profoundly uneasy.

RUTH (*sitting in the armchair*) Perhaps there's something pressing on your brain.

CHARLES. If there were something pressing on my brain I should have violent headaches, shouldn't I?

RUTH. Not necessarily. An uncle of mine had a lump the size of a cricket ball pressing on his brain for years and he never felt a thing.

CHARLES. I know I should know if I had anything like that. (*He rises and goes over to the fireplace*)

RUTH. He didn't.

CHARLES. What happened to him?

RUTH. He had it taken out and he's been as bright as a button ever since.

CHARLES. Did he have any sort of delusions? Did he think he saw things that weren't there?

RUTH. No, I don't think so.

CHARLES. Well, what the hell are we talking about him for then? It's sheer waste of valuable time.

RUTH. I only brought him up as an example.

CHARLES. I think I'm going mad.

RUTH. How do you feel now?

CHARLES. Physically, do you mean?

RUTH. Altogether.

CHARLES (*after due reflection*) Apart from being worried, I feel quite normal.

RUTH. Good. You're not hearing or seeing anything in the least unusual?

CHARLES. Not a thing.

(*Light Cue No. 3. Act II, Scene 1*)

(ELVIRA *enters by the windows, carrying a bunch of grey roses. She crosses to the writing-table upstage* R, *and throws the zinnias into the waste-paper basket and puts her roses into the vase. The roses are as grey as the rest of her*)

ELVIRA. You've absolutely ruined that border by the sundial. It looks like a mixed salad.

CHARLES. Oh, my God!

RUTH. What's the matter now?

CHARLES. She's here again!

RUTH. What do you mean? Who's here again?

CHARLES. Elvira.

RUTH. Pull yourself together and don't be absurd.

ELVIRA. It's all those nasturtiums; they're so vulgar.

CHARLES. I like nasturtiums.

RUTH. You like what?

ELVIRA (*putting her grey roses into the vase*) They're all right in moderation, but in a mass like that they look beastly.

CHARLES (*crossing over to* R *of Ruth,* C) Help me, Ruth—you've got to help me——

RUTH (*rising and retreating a pace to* L) What did you mean about nasturtiums?

CHARLES (*taking Ruth's hands and coming round to the* L *of her*) Never mind about that now. I tell you she's here again.

ELVIRA (*coming to above the sofa*) You have been having a nice scene, haven't you? I could hear you right down the garden.

CHARLES. Please mind your own business.

RUTH. If you behaving like a lunatic isn't my business, nothing is.

ELVIRA. I expect it was about me, wasn't it? I know I ought to feel sorry, but I'm not. I'm delighted.

CHARLES. How can you be so inconsiderate?

RUTH (*shrilly*) Inconsiderate! I like that, I must say!

CHARLES. Ruth—darling—please . . .

RUTH. I've done everything I can to help. I've controlled myself admirably. And I should like to say here and now that I don't believe a word about your damned hallucination. You're up to something, Charles—there's been a certain furtiveness in your manner for weeks. Why don't you be honest and tell me what it is?

CHARLES. You're wrong—you're dead wrong! I haven't been in the least furtive—I——

RUTH. You're trying to upset me. (*She moves away from Charles*) For some obscure reason you're trying to goad me into doing something that I might regret. (*She bursts into tears*) I won't stand for it any more. You're making me utterly miserable! (*She crosses to the sofa and falls into the* ʀ *end of it*)

Cʜᴀʀʟᴇs (*crosses to Ruth*) Ruth—please——

Rᴜᴛʜ. Don't come near me!

Eʟᴠɪʀᴀ. Let her have a nice cry. It'll do her good. (*She saunters round to downstage* ʟ)

Cʜᴀʀʟᴇs. You're utterly heartless!

Rᴜᴛʜ. Heartless!

Cʜᴀʀʟᴇs (*wildly*) I was not talking to you! I was talking to Elvira.

Rᴜᴛʜ. Go on talking to her then, talk to her until you're blue in the face, but don't talk to me.

Cʜᴀʀʟᴇs (*crossing to Elvira*) Help me, Elvira——

Eʟᴠɪʀᴀ. How?

Cʜᴀʀʟᴇs. Make her see you or something.

Eʟᴠɪʀᴀ. I'm afraid I couldn't manage that. It's technically the most difficult business—frightfully complicated, you know—it takes years of study——

Cʜᴀʀʟᴇs. You are here, aren't you? You're not an illusion?

Eʟᴠɪʀᴀ. I may be an illusion, but I'm most definitely here.

Cʜᴀʀʟᴇs. How did you get here?

Eʟᴠɪʀᴀ. I told you last night—I don't exactly know——

Cʜᴀʀʟᴇs. Well, you must make me a promise that in future you only come and talk to me when I'm alone.

Eʟᴠɪʀᴀ (*pouting*) How unkind you are, making me feel so unwanted. I've never been treated so rudely.

Cʜᴀʀʟᴇs. I don't mean to be rude, but you must see——

Eʟᴠɪʀᴀ. It's all your own fault for having married a woman who is incapable of seeing beyond the nose on her face. If she had a grain of real sympathy or affection for you she'd believe what you tell her.

Cʜᴀʀʟᴇs. How could you expect anybody to believe this?

Eʟᴠɪʀᴀ. You'd be surprised how gullible people are; we often laugh about it on the Other Side.

(Rᴜᴛʜ, *who has stopped crying and been staring at Charles in horror, suddenly rises*)

Rᴜᴛʜ (*gently*) Charles!

Cʜᴀʀʟᴇs (*surprised at her tone*) Yes, dear——

(Cʜᴀʀʟᴇs *crosses to her,* ʀ)

Rᴜᴛʜ. I'm awfully sorry I was cross.

Cʜᴀʀʟᴇs. But, my dear——

Rᴜᴛʜ. I understand everything now. I do really.

Cʜᴀʀʟᴇs. You do?

Rᴜᴛʜ (*patting his arm reassuringly*) Of course I do.

Eʟᴠɪʀᴀ. Look out—she's up to something.

Cʜᴀʀʟᴇs. Will you please be quiet?

RUTH. Of course, darling. We'll all be quiet, won't we? We'll be as quiet as little mice.

CHARLES. Ruth dear, listen——

RUTH. I want you to come upstairs with me and go to bed.

ELVIRA. The way that woman harps on bed is nothing short of erotic.

CHARLES. I'll deal with you later.

RUTH. Very well, darling—come along.

CHARLES. What are you up to?

RUTH. I'm not up to anything. I just want you to go quietly to bed and wait there until Doctor Bradman comes.

CHARLES. No, Ruth, you're wrong——

RUTH (*firmly*) Come, dear——

ELVIRA. She'll have you in a strait-jacket before you know where you are.

CHARLES (*coming to Elvira—frantically*) Help me—you must help me——

ELVIRA (*enjoying herself*) My dear, I would with pleasure, but I can't think how.

CHARLES. I can. (*He moves back to Ruth*) Listen, Ruth——

RUTH. Yes, dear?

CHARLES. If I promise to go to bed, will you let me stay here for five minutes longer?

RUTH. I really think it would be better——

CHARLES. Bear with me, however mad it may seem, bear with me for just five minutes longer.

RUTH (*leaving go of him*) Very well. What is it?

CHARLES. Sit down.

RUTH (*sitting down*) All right. There!

CHARLES. Now listen, listen carefully——

ELVIRA. Have a cigarette; it will soothe your nerves.

CHARLES. I don't want a cigarette.

RUTH (*indulgently*) Then you shan't have one, darling.

CHARLES. Ruth, I want to explain to you clearly and without emotion that beyond any shadow of doubt, the ghost or shade or whatever you like to call it of my first wife Elvira is in this room now.

RUTH. Yes, dear.

CHARLES. I know you don't believe it and are trying valiantly to humour me, but I intend to prove it to you.

RUTH. Why not lie down and have a nice rest and you can prove anything you want to later on?

CHARLES. She may not be here later on.

ELVIRA. Don't worry—she will!

CHARLES. Oh God!

RUTH. Hush, dear.

CHARLES (*to Elvira*) Promise you'll do what I ask?

ELVIRA. That all depends what it is.

CHARLES (*between them both, facing up stage*) Ruth—you see that bowl of flowers on the piano?

RUTH. Yes, dear, I did it myself this morning.

ELVIRA. Very untidily, if I may say so.

CHARLES. You may not.

RUTH. Very well—I never will again. I promise.

CHARLES. Elvira will now carry that bowl of flowers to the mantelpiece and back again. You will, Elvira, won't you? Just to please me.

ELVIRA. I don't really see why I should. You've been quite insufferable to me ever since I materialized.

CHARLES. Please!

ELVIRA (*going over to the piano*) All right, I will just this once. Not that I approve of all these Maskelyne and Devant carryings-on.

CHARLES (*crossing to the mantelpiece*) Now, Ruth—watch carefully!

RUTH (*patiently*) Very well, dear.

CHARLES. Go on, Elvira—take it to the mantelpiece and back again.

(ELVIRA *takes a bowl of pansies off the piano and brings it slowly down stage, below the armchair to the fire; then suddenly pushes it towards Ruth's face, who jumps up and faces Charles, who is at the mantelpiece*)

RUTH (*furiously*) How dare you, Charles! You ought to be ashamed of yourself.

CHARLES. What on earth for?

RUTH (*hysterically*) It's a trick. I know perfectly well it's a trick. You've been working up to this. It's all part of some horrible plan . . .

CHARLES. It isn't—I swear it isn't. Elvira—do something else, for God's sake!

ELVIRA. Certainly—anything to oblige.

RUTH (*becoming really frightened*) You want to get rid of me— you're trying to drive me out of my mind——

CHARLES. Don't be so silly.

RUTH. You're cruel and sadistic and I'll never forgive you.

(ELVIRA *picks up the chair from downstage* L, *holds it in mid-air as if to hit Ruth,* RUTH *flinches, then* ELVIRA *puts it back, and stands above the windows.* RUTH *makes a dive for the door, moving between the armchair and sofa.* CHARLES *follows and catches her*)

I'm not going to put up with this any more.

CHARLES (*holding her*) You must believe it—you must——

RUTH. Let me go immediately.

CHARLES. That was Elvira—I swear it was.

RUTH (*struggling*) Let me go.

CHARLES. Ruth—please——

(RUTH *breaks away to the windows.* ELVIRA *shuts them in her face and crosses quickly to the mantelpiece.* RUTH *turns at the windows to face Charles*)

RUTH (*looking at Charles with eyes of horror*) Charles—this is madness—sheer madness—it's some sort of auto-suggestion, isn't it?—some form of hypnotism, swear to me it's only that—(*rushing to Charles,* C) swear to me it's only that.

ELVIRA (*taking an expensive vase from the mantelpiece and crashing it into the grate*) Hypnotism my foot!

(RUTH *gives a scream and goes into violent hysterics*)

(*Light Cue No. 4. Act II, Scene 1*)

The CURTAIN *falls*

SCENE 2

The time is late on the following afternoon. The doors are shut. The windows are shut. The curtains are open.

(*Light Cue No. 1. Act II, Scene 2*)

When the CURTAIN *rises* RUTH *is sitting alone at the tea-table, which is set in front of the fire. After a moment or two she gets up and, frowning thoughtfully, goes to the mantelpiece and takes a cigarette out of a box and lights it. As she returns to the table, the front-door bell rings. She hears it and straightens herself as though preparing for a difficult interview.*

EDITH *enters.*

EDITH. Madame Arcati.

(EDITH *steps aside and* MADAME ARCATI *comes in. Madame Arcati is wearing a tweed coat and skirt, and a great many amber beads and, possibly, a beret. She goes to Ruth, who is standing below the sofa between the sofa and the armchair.* EDITH *goes out*)

MADAME ARCATI. My dear Mrs Condomine, I came directly I got your message.

RUTH. That was very kind of you.

MADAME ARCATI (*briskly*) Kind?—nonsense. Nothing kind about it. I look upon it as an outing.

RUTH. I'm so glad. Will you have some tea?

MADAME ARCATI. China or Indian?

RUTH. China.

MADAME ARCATI. Good. I never touch Indian; it upsets my vibrations.

RUTH. Do sit down.

(Ruth *sits at the* L *end of the sofa and pours out tea.* Madame Arcati *sits in the armchair*)

Madame Arcati (*turning her head and sniffing*) I find this room very interesting—very interesting indeed. I noticed it the other night.

Ruth. I'm not entirely surprised. (*She proceeds to pour out tea*)

Madame Arcati (*pulling off her gloves*) Have you ever been to Cowden Manor?

Ruth. No, I'm afraid I haven't.

Madame Arcati. That's very interesting too. Strikes you like a blow between the eyes the moment you walk into the drawing-room. Two lumps of sugar, please, and no milk at all.

Ruth. I am profoundly disturbed, Madame Arcati, and I want your help.

Madame Arcati. Aha! I thought as much. What's in these sandwiches?

Ruth. Cucumber.

Madame Arcati. Couldn't be better. (*She takes one*) Fire away.

Ruth. It's most awfully difficult to explain.

Madame Arcati. Facts first—explanations afterwards.

Ruth. It's the facts that are difficult to explain. They're so fantastic.

Madame Arcati. Facts very often are. Take creative talent, for instance, how do you account for that? Look at Shakespeare and Michelangelo! Try to explain Mozart snatching sounds out of the air and putting them down on paper when he was practically a baby—facts—plain facts. I know it's the fashion nowadays to ascribe it all to glands, but my reply to that is fiddlededee.

Ruth. Yes, I'm sure you're quite right.

Madame Arcati. There are more things in heaven and earth than are dreamt of in your philosophy, Mrs Condomine.

Ruth. There certainly are.

Madame Arcati. Come now—take the plunge—out with it. You've heard strange noises in the night, no doubt. Boards creaking—doors slamming—subdued moaning in the passages. Is that it?

Ruth. No—I'm afraid it isn't.

Madame Arcati. No sudden gusts of cold wind, I hope?

Ruth. No, it's worse than that.

Madame Arcati. I'm all attention.

Ruth (*with an effort*) I know it sounds idiotic, but the other night—during the séance—something happened.

Madame Arcati. I knew it! Probably a poltergeist; they're enormously cunning, you know; they sometimes lie doggo for days.

Ruth. You know that my husband was married before?

Madame Arcati. Yes, I have heard it mentioned.

RUTH. His first wife, Elvira, died comparatively young.

MADAME ARCATI (*sharply*) Where?

RUTH. Here—in this house—in this very room.

MADAME ARCATI (*whistling*) Whew! I'm beginning to see daylight.

RUTH. She was convalescing after pneumonia and one evening she started to laugh helplessly at one of the B.B.C. musical programmes and died of a heart attack.

MADAME ARCATI. And she materialized the other evening—after I had gone?

RUTH. Not to me, but to my husband.

(MADAME ARCATI *rises, crosses upstage* L, *then across to the fire below the sofa and to the windows again, above the sofa*)

MADAME ARCATI (*impulsively*) Capital! Capital! Oh, but that's splendid!

RUTH (*coldly*) From your own professional standpoint I can see that it might be regarded as a major achievement.

MADAME ARCATI (*delighted*) A triumph, my dear! Nothing more nor less than a triumph!

RUTH. But from my own personal point of view it is, to say the least of it, embarrassing.

MADAME ARCATI (*walking about the room*) At last! At last! A genuine materialization!

RUTH. Please sit down again, Madame Arcati . . .

MADAME ARCATI. How could anyone sit down at a moment like this? It's tremendous! I haven't had such a success since the Sudbury case.

RUTH (*sharply*) Nevertheless, I must insist upon you sitting down and controlling your natural exuberance. I appreciate fully your pride in your achievement, but I would like to point out that it has made my position in this house untenable and that I hold you entirely responsible.

MADAME ARCATI (*coming to the armchair and sitting; contrite*) Forgive me, Mrs Condomine. I am being abominably selfish. How can I help you?

RUTH. How? By sending her back immediately to where she came from, of course.

MADAME ARCATI. I'm afraid that that is easier said than done.

RUTH. Do you mean to tell me that she is liable to stay here indefinitely?

MADAME ARCATI. It's difficult to say. I fear it depends largely on her.

RUTH. But my dear Madame Arcati . . .

MADAME ARCATI. Where is she now?

RUTH. My husband has driven her into Folkestone. Apparently she was anxious to see an old friend of hers who is staying at the Grand.

(MADAME ARCATI *produces a note-book from her bag and takes notes through the following speeches*)

MADAME ARCATI. Forgive this formality, but I shall have to make a report to the Psychical Research people.

RUTH. I would be very much obliged if there were no names mentioned.

MADAME ARCATI. The report will be confidential.

RUTH. This is a small village, you know, and gossip would be most undesirable.

MADAME ARCATI. I quite understand. You say she is visible only to your husband?

RUTH. Yes.

MADAME ARCATI. Visible only to husband. Audible too, I presume?

RUTH. Extremely audible.

MADAME ARCATI. Extremely audible. Your husband was devoted to her?

RUTH (*with slight irritation*) I believe so!

MADAME ARCATI. Husband devoted.

RUTH. It was apparently a reasonably happy marriage . . .

MADAME ARCATI. Oh, tut tut!

RUTH. I beg your pardon?

MADAME ARCATI. When did she pass over?

RUTH. Seven years ago.

MADAME ARCATI. Aha! That means she must have been on the waiting list.

RUTH. Waiting list?

MADAME ARCATI. Yes, otherwise she would have got beyond the materialization stage by now. She must have marked herself down for a return visit and she'd never have been able to manage it unless there was a strong influence at work.

RUTH. Do you mean that Charles—my husband—wanted her back all that much?

MADAME ARCATI. Possibly, or it might have been her own determination.

RUTH. That sounds much more likely.

MADAME ARCATI. Would you say that she was a woman of strong character?

RUTH (*with rising annoyance*) I really don't know, Madame Arcati—I never met her. Nor am I particularly interested in how and why she got here. I am solely concerned with the question of how to get her away again as soon as possible.

MADAME ARCATI. I fully sympathize with you, Mrs Condomine, and I assure you I will do anything in my power to help. But at the moment I fear I cannot offer any great hopes.

RUTH. But I always understood that there was a way of exorcizing ghosts, some sort of ritual?

MADAME ARCATI. You mean the old Bell and Book method?

RUTH. Yes—I suppose I do.

MADAME ARCATI. Poppycock, Mrs Condomine! It was quite effective in the old days of genuine religious belief, but that's all changed now. I believe the decline of faith in the Spirit World has been causing grave concern.

RUTH (*impatiently*) Has it indeed?

MADAME ARCATI. There was a time of course when a drop of holy water could send even a poltergeist scampering for cover, but not any more. 'Ou sont les neiges d'Antan?'

RUTH. Be that as it may, Madame Arcati, I must beg of you to do your utmost to dematerialize my husband's first wife as soon as possible.

MADAME ARCATI. The time has come for me to admit to you frankly, Mrs Condomine, that I haven't the faintest idea how to set about it.

RUTH (*rising*) Do you mean to sit there and tell me that having mischievously conjured up this ghost or spirit, or whatever she is, and placed me in a hideous position, you are unable to do anything about it at all?

MADAME ARCATI. Honesty is the best policy.

RUTH. But it's outrageous! I ought to hand you over to the police. (*She crosses to the fireplace*)

MADAME ARCATI. You go too far, Mrs Condomine.

RUTH (*furiously*) I go too far indeed! Do you realize what your insane amateur muddling has done?

MADAME ARCATI. I have been a professional since I was a child, Mrs Condomine. 'Amateur' is a word I cannot tolerate.

RUTH. It seems to me to be the height of amateurishness to evoke malignant spirits and not be able to get rid of them again.

MADAME ARCATI (*with dignity*) I was in a trance. Anything might happen when I am in a trance.

RUTH. Well, all I can suggest is that you go into another one immediately and get this damned woman out of my house.

MADAME ARCATI. I can't go into trances at a moment's notice. It takes hours of preparation. In addition to which I have to be extremely careful of my diet for days beforehand. Today, for instance, I happened to lunch with friends and had pigeon pie which, plus these cucumber sandwiches, would make a trance out of the question.

RUTH. Well, you'll have to do something.

MADAME ARCATI. I will report the whole matter to the Society for Psychical Research at the earliest possible moment.

RUTH. Will they be able to do anything?

MADAME ARCATI. I doubt it. They'd send an investigation committee, I expect, and do a lot of questioning and wall-tapping and mumbo-jumbo, and then they'd have a conference and you would probably have to go up to London to testify.

RUTH (*near tears*) It's too humiliating—it really is.

MADAME ARCATI (*rising and going to Ruth at the fireplace*) Please try not to upset yourself. Nothing can be achieved by upsetting yourself.

RUTH. It's all very fine for you to talk like this, Madame Arcati. You don't seem to have the faintest realization of my position.

MADAME ARCATI. Try to look on the bright side.

RUTH. Bright side indeed! If your husband's first wife suddenly appeared from the grave and came to live in the house with you, do you suppose you'd be able to look on the bright side?

MADAME ARCATI (*crossing away to L and up to C*) I resent your tone, Mrs Condomine; I really do.

RUTH. You most decidedly have no right to. You are entirely to blame for the whole horrible situation.

MADAME ARCATI. Kindly remember that I came here the other night on your own invitation.

RUTH. On my husband's invitation.

MADAME ARCATI. I did what I was requested to do, which was to give a séance and establish contact with the Other Side. I had no idea that there was any ulterior motive mixed up with it.

RUTH. Ulterior motive?

MADAME ARCATI. Your husband was obviously eager to get in touch with his former wife. If I had been aware of that at the time I should naturally have consulted you beforehand. After all, 'Noblesse oblige'!

RUTH. He had no intention of trying to get in touch with anyone. The whole thing was planned in order for him to get material for a mystery story he is writing about a homicidal medium.

MADAME ARCATI (*drawing herself up*) Am I to understand that I was only invited in a spirit of mockery?

RUTH. Not at all. He merely wanted to make notes of some of the tricks of the trade.

MADAME ARCATI (*incensed*) Tricks of the trade! Insufferable! I've never been so insulted in my life. I feel we have nothing more to say to one another, Mrs Condomine. Goodbye! (*She turns away up stage C to the door*)

RUTH. Please don't go—please——

MADAME ARCATI (*turning and facing Ruth upstage C by the door*) Your attitude from the outset has been most unpleasant, Mrs Condomine. Some of your remarks have been discourteous in the extreme and I should like to say, without umbrage, that if you and your husband were foolish enough to tamper with the unseen for paltry motives and in a spirit of ribaldry, whatever has happened to you is your own fault, and, to coin a phrase, as far as I'm concerned you can stew in your own juice!

(Madame Arcati *goes majestically from the room*)

Ruth (*stubbing out her cigarette in the ashtray on the small table downstage* R) Damn—Damn—Damn!

(*After a moment or two* Charles *comes in with* Elvira)

(*Light Cue No. 2. Act II, Scene 2*)

(Charles *moves to above the sofa.* Elvira *turns to the piano and tidies her hair in the mirror*)

Charles. What on earth was Madame Arcati doing here?

Ruth. She came to tea.

Charles. Did you ask her?

Ruth. Of course I did.

Charles. You never told me you were going to.

Ruth. You never told me you were going to ask Elvira to live with us.

Charles. I didn't.

Elvira (*sauntering over to the tea-table*) Oh, yes, you did, darling —it was your subconscious.

Charles. What was the old girl so cross about? She practically cut me dead.

Ruth. I told her the truth, about why we invited her the other night.

Charles. That was quite unnecessary and most unkind.

Ruth. She needed taking down a bit, she was blowing herself out like a pouter pigeon.

Charles. Why did you ask her to tea?

Elvira (*having moved over to above the armchair; leaning on the back*) To get me exorcized, of course. Oh dear, I wish I could have a cucumber sandwich. I did love them so.

Charles. Is that true, Ruth?

Ruth. Is what true?

Charles. What Elvira said.

Ruth. You know perfectly well I can't hear what Elvira says.

Charles. She said that you got Madame Arcati here to try to get her exorcized. Is that true?

Ruth. We discussed the possibilities.

Elvira (*sitting in the armchair, her legs over the left arm*) There's a snake in the grass for you.

Charles. You had no right to do such a thing without consulting me.

Ruth. I have every right. This situation is absolutely impossible, and you know it.

Charles. If only you'd make an effort and try to be a little more friendly to Elvira we might all have quite a jolly time.

Ruth. I have no wish to have a jolly time with Elvira.

Elvira. She's certainly very bad tempered, isn't she? I can't think why you married her.

CHARLES. She's naturally a bit upset—we must make allowances.

ELVIRA. I was never bad tempered though, was I, darling? Not even when you were beastly to me.

CHARLES. I was never beastly to you.

RUTH (*exasperated*) Where is Elvira at the moment?

CHARLES. In the chair by the table.

RUTH (*crossing and sitting at the L end of the sofa; pointing at Elvira*) Now look here, Elvira—I shall have to call you Elvira, shan't I? I can't very well go on saying Mrs Condomine all the time, it would sound too silly.

ELVIRA. I don't see why.

RUTH. Did she say anything?

CHARLES. She said she'd like nothing better.

ELVIRA (*giggling*) You really are sweet, Charles darling. I worship you.

RUTH. I wish to be absolutely honest with you, Elvira——

ELVIRA. Hold on to your hats, boys!

RUTH. I admit I did ask Madame Arcati here with a view to getting you exorcized; and I think that if you were in my position you'd have done exactly the same thing—wouldn't you?

ELVIRA. I shouldn't have done it so obviously.

RUTH. What did she say?

CHARLES. Nothing. She just nodded and smiled.

RUTH (*with a forced smile*) Thank you, Elvira; that's generous of you. I really would so much rather that there were no misunderstandings between us.

CHARLES. That's very sensible, Ruth—I agree entirely.

RUTH (*to Elvira*) I want, before we go any further, to ask you a frank question. Why did you really come here? I don't see that you could have hoped to have achieved anything by it beyond the immediate joke of making Charles into a sort of astral bigamist.

ELVIRA. I came because the power of Charles's love tugged and tugged and tugged at me.

(CHARLES *chuckles in self-satisfaction*)

Didn't it, my sweet?

RUTH. What did she say?

CHARLES. She said that she came because she wanted to see me again.

RUTH. Well, she's done that now, hasn't she?

CHARLES. We can't be inhospitable, Ruth.

RUTH. I have no wish to be inhospitable; but I should like to have just an idea of how long you intend to stay, Elvira?

ELVIRA. I don't know—I really don't know! (*She giggles*) Isn't it awful?

CHARLES. She says she doesn't know.

RUTH. Surely that's a little inconsiderate?

ELVIRA. Didn't the old spiritualist have any constructive ideas about getting rid of me?

CHARLES. What did Madame Arcati say?

RUTH. She said she couldn't do a thing.

ELVIRA (*rising and crossing to the window*) Hurray!

CHARLES. Don't be upset, Ruth dear—we shall soon adjust ourselves, you know. You must admit it's a unique experience. I can see no valid reason why we shouldn't get a great deal of fun out of it.

RUTH. Fun! Charles, how can you—you must be out of your mind!

CHARLES (*crossing below the sofa to the fireplace*) Not at all—I thought I was at first—but now I must say I'm beginning to enjoy myself.

RUTH (*bursting into tears*) Oh, Charles—Charles——

ELVIRA. She's off again.

CHARLES. You really must not be so callous, Elvira. Try to see her point a little.

RUTH. I suppose she said something insulting.

CHARLES. No, dear, she didn't do anything of the sort.

RUTH. Now look here, Elvira . . .

CHARLES. She's over by the window now.

RUTH. Why the hell can't she stay in the same place?

ELVIRA. Temper again! My poor Charles, what a terrible life you must lead!

CHARLES. Do shut up, darling, you'll only make everything worse.

RUTH. Who was that 'darling' addressed to—her or me?

CHARLES. Both of you.

(RUTH *rises*. ELVIRA *drops downstage* L *to the gramophone*)

RUTH (*stamping her foot*) This is intolerable!

CHARLES. For Heaven's sake don't get into another state.

RUTH (*furiously*) I've been doing my level best to control myself ever since yesterday morning, and I'm damned if I'm going to try any more, the strain is too much. She has the advantage of being able to say whatever she pleases without me being able to hear her, but she can hear me all right, can't she, without any modified interpreting?

CHARLES. Modified interpreting! I don't know what you mean.

RUTH. Oh, yes, you do—you haven't told me once what she really said—you wouldn't dare. Judging from her photograph she's the type who would use most unpleasant language.

CHARLES. Ruth—you're not to talk like that.

RUTH. I've been making polite conversation all through dinner last night and breakfast and lunch today—and it's been a nightmare—and I am not going to do it any more. (*She moves to the* L *of the armchair*) I don't like Elvira any more than she likes me, and what's more, I'm certain that I never could have, dead or alive. (*Going up stage a pace she turns to face Charles, at the fire*) If, since her untimely arrival here the other evening, she had shown the slightest sign of good manners, the slightest sign of breeding, I might have felt differently towards her, but all she has done is try to make mischief between us and have private jokes with you against me. I am now going up to my room and I shall have my dinner on a tray. You and she can have the house to yourselves and joke and gossip with each other to your heart's content. (*Spoken in the doorway*) The first thing in the morning I am going up to London to interview the Psychical Research Society, and if they fail me I shall go straight to the Archbishop of Canterbury. . . .

(RUTH *exits*)

CHARLES (*moving up stage to* C, *to follow her*) Ruth . . .

ELVIRA (*crossing over to the fireplace*) Let her go. She'll calm down later on.

CHARLES. It's unlike her to behave like this. She's generally so equable.

ELVIRA. No, she isn't. Not really. Her mouth gives her away. It's a hard mouth, Charles.

CHARLES (*coming downstage* C *between the armchair and the sofa*) Her mouth's got nothing to do with it. I resent you discussing Ruth as though she were a horse.

ELVIRA. Do you love her?

CHARLES. Of course I do.

ELVIRA. As much as you loved me?

CHARLES. Don't be silly—it's all entirely different.

ELVIRA. I'm so glad. Nothing could ever have been quite the same, could it?

CHARLES. You always behaved very badly.

ELVIRA. Oh, Charles!

CHARLES. I'm grieved to see that your sojourn in the other world hasn't improved you in the least.

ELVIRA (*curling up in* R *end of the sofa*) Go on, darling—I love it when you pretend to be cross with me.

CHARLES. I'm now going up to talk to Ruth.

ELVIRA. Cowardy custard.

CHARLES. Don't be idiotic. I can't let her go like that. I must be a little nice and sympathetic to her.

ELVIRA. I don't see why! If she's set on being disagreeable, I should just let her get on with it.

CHARLES. The whole business is very difficult for her—we must be fair.

ELVIRA. She should learn to be more adaptable.

CHARLES. She probably will in time—it's been a shock——

ELVIRA. Has it been a shock for you too, darling?

CHARLES. Of course! What did you expect?

ELVIRA. A nice shock?

CHARLES. What do you want, Elvira?

ELVIRA. Want? I don't know what you mean.

CHARLES. I remember that whenever you were overpoweringly demure it usually meant that you wanted something.

ELVIRA. It's horrid of you to be so suspicious. All I want is to be with you.

CHARLES. Well, you are.

ELVIRA. I mean alone, darling. If you go and pamper Ruth and smarm her over, she'll probably come flouncing down again and our lovely quiet evening together will be spoilt.

CHARLES. You're incorrigibly selfish.

ELVIRA. Well, I haven't seen you for seven years—it's only natural that I should want a little time alone with you—to talk over old times. I'll let you go up just for a little while if you really think it's your duty.

CHARLES. Of course it is.

ELVIRA (smiling) Then I don't mind.

CHARLES. You're disgraceful, Elvira.

ELVIRA. You won't be long, will you? You'll come down again very soon?

CHARLES. I shall probably dress for dinner while I'm upstairs. You can read the *Tatler* or something.

ELVIRA. Darling, you don't have to dress—for me.

CHARLES. I always dress for dinner.

ELVIRA. What are you going to have? I should like to watch you eat something really delicious.

CHARLES (moving up to the door) Be a good girl now—you can play the gramophone if you like.

ELVIRA (demurely) Thank you, Charles.

> (CHARLES goes out.
>
> ELVIRA gets up, looks in the gramophone cupboard, finds the record of 'Always' and puts it on. She starts to waltz lightly round the room to it.
>
> EDITH comes in to fetch the tea-tray. She sees the gramophone playing by itself and so she turns it off and puts the record back in the cupboard. While she is picking up the tray, ELVIRA takes the record out and puts it on again. EDITH gives a shriek, drops the tray and rushes out of the room. ELVIRA continues to waltz gaily)

(Light Cue No. 3. Act II, Scene 2)

CURTAIN

SCENE 3

The Time is evening several days later. The doors are shut. The windows are also shut. The curtains are open.

(Light Cue No. 1. Act II, Scene 3)

When the CURTAIN *rises,* MRS BRADMAN *is sitting in the armchair.* RUTH *is standing by the window drumming on the pane with her fingers.*

MRS BRADMAN. Does it show any signs of clearing?

RUTH. No, it's still pouring.

MRS BRADMAN. I do sympathize with you, really I do. It's really been quite a chapter of accidents, hasn't it?

RUTH. It certainly has.

MRS BRADMAN. That happens sometimes, you know. Everything seems to go wrong at once. Exactly as though there were some evil forces at work.

*(*RUTH *comes down to the gramophone)*

I remember once when George and I went away for a fortnight's holiday, not long after we were married, we were dogged by bad luck from beginning to end. The weather was vile—George sprained his ankle—I caught a cold and had to stay in bed for two days—and to crown everything the lamp fell over in the sitting-room and set fire to the treatise George had written on hyperplasia of the abdominal glands.

RUTH *(absently)* How dreadful! *(She wanders up stage a little)*

MRS BRADMAN. He had to write it all over again, every single word.

RUTH. You're sure you wouldn't like a cocktail or some sherry or anything?

MRS BRADMAN. No, thank you—really not. George will be down in a minute and we've got to go like lightning. We were supposed to be at the Wilmots' at seven and it's nearly that now.

RUTH *(coming away from the window)* I think I'll have a little sherry. I feel I need it. *(She moves upstage* R *to the drinks table and pours out sherry)*

MRS BRADMAN. Don't worry about your husband's arm, Mrs Condomine. I'm sure it's only a sprain.

RUTH. It's not his arm I'm worried about.

MRS BRADMAN. And I'm sure Edith will be up and about again in a few days.

RUTH. My cook gave notice this morning. *(She comes down to the fireplace)*

MRS BRADMAN. Well, really! Servants are awful, aren't they? Not a shred of gratitude. At the first sign of trouble they run out on you—like rats leaving a sinking ship.

RUTH. I can't feel that your simile was entirely fortunate, Mrs Bradman.

MRS BRADMAN (*flustered*) Oh, I didn't mean that, really I didn't!

(DR BRADMAN *comes in*)

DR BRADMAN (*above the sofa*) Nothing to worry about, Mrs Condomine—it's only a slight strain.

RUTH. I'm so relieved.

DR BRADMAN. He made a good deal of fuss when I examined it. Men are much worse patients than women, you know—particularly highly-strung men like your husband.

RUTH. Is he highly strung, do you think?

DR BRADMAN. Yes. As a matter of fact I wanted to talk to you about that. I'm afraid he's been overworking lately.

RUTH (*frowning*) Overworking?

DR BRADMAN. He's in rather a nervous condition—nothing serious, you understand——

RUTH. What makes you think so?

DR BRADMAN. I know the symptoms. Of course the shock of his fall might have something to do with it, but I certainly should advise a complete rest for a couple of weeks.

RUTH. You mean he ought to go away?

DR BRADMAN. I do. In cases like that a change of atmosphere can work wonders.

RUTH. What symptoms did you notice?

DR BRADMAN. Oh, nothing to be unduly alarmed about—a certain air of strain—an inability to focus his eyes on the person he is talking to—a few rather marked irrelevancies in his conversation.

RUTH. I see. Can you remember any specific example?

DR BRADMAN. Oh, he suddenly shouted, 'What are you doing in the bathroom?' and then a little later, while I was writing him a prescription, he suddenly said, 'For God's sake behave yourself!'

MRS BRADMAN. How extraordinary.

RUTH (*nervously*) He often goes on like that. Particularly when he's immersed in writing a book.

DR BRADMAN. Oh, I am not in the least perturbed about it really—but I do think a rest and a change would be a good idea.

RUTH. Thank you so much, Doctor. Would you like some sherry?

DR BRADMAN. No, thank you. We really must be off.

RUTH. How is poor Edith?

DR BRADMAN. She'll be all right in a few days. She's still recovering from the concussion.

MRS BRADMAN. It's funny, isn't it, that both your housemaid and your husband should fall down on the same day, isn't it?

RUTH. Yes, if that sort of thing amuses you.

Mrs Bradman (*giggling nervously*) Of course I didn't mean it like that, Mrs Condomine.

Dr Bradman. Come along, my dear. You're talking too much as usual.

Mrs Bradman. You are horrid, George.

(Mrs Bradman *rises and crosses to* Ruth rc *below the sofa. Both* Bradmans *move up to the door*)

Good-bye, Mrs Condomine.

Ruth (*shaking hands*) Good-bye.

Dr Bradman (*also shaking hands*) I'll pop in and have a look at both patients some time tomorrow morning.

Ruth. Thank you so much.

(*Light Cue No. 2. Act II, Scene 3*)

(Charles *comes in and to above the table* c. *His left arm is in a sling.* Elvira *follows him in and crosses above the sofa to the fire and then across the front to* lc. Ruth *is at the mantelpiece*)

Dr Bradman. Well—how does it feel?

Charles. All right.

Dr Bradman. It's only a slight sprain, you know.

Charles. Is this damned sling really essential?

Dr Bradman. It's a wise precaution. It will prevent you using your left hand except when it's really necessary.

Charles. I had intended to drive into Folkestone this evening.

Dr Bradman. It would be much better if you didn't.

Charles. It's extremely inconvenient.

Ruth. You can easily wait and go tomorrow, Charles.

Elvira. I can't stand another of those dreary evenings at home, Charles. It'll drive me dotty. And I haven't seen a movie for seven years.

Charles (*crossing below Mrs Bradman to the* r *of Elvira*) Let me be the first to congratulate you.

Dr Bradman (*kindly*) What's that, old man?

Ruth (*with intense meaning*) Charles, dear, try to be sensible, I implore you!

Charles. Sorry—I forgot.

Dr Bradman. You can drive the car if you promise to go very slowly and carefully. Your gear change is on the right, isn't it?

Charles. Yes.

Dr Bradman. Well, use your left hand as little as possible.

Charles. All right.

Ruth. You'd much better stay at home.

Dr Bradman. Couldn't you drive him in?

Ruth (*stiffly*) I'm afraid not. I have lots to do in the house, and there's Edith to be attended to.

Dr Bradman. Well, I'll leave you to fight it out among yourselves. (*To Charles*) But remember, if you do insist on going—carefully does it. The roads are very slippery anyhow. Come along, Violet.

MRS BRADMAN. Good-bye again. Good-bye, Mr Condomine.

CHARLES. Good-bye.

(CHARLES *follows the* BRADMANS *off*)

RUTH (*left alone, at the fire, speaking to Elvira*) You really are infuriating, Elvira. Surely you could wait and go to the movies another night.

(ELVIRA *takes a rose out of the vase on the* o *table and throws it at Ruth. Then she runs out of the windows*)

(*Light Cue No. 3. Act II, Scene 3*)

(*Catching the rose*) And stop behaving like a schoolgirl. You're old enough to know better.

CHARLES (*coming in to* C) What?

RUTH. I was talking to Elvira.

CHARLES. She isn't here.

RUTH. She was a moment ago. (*She puts the rose back in the vase*) She threw a rose at me.

CHARLES (*going to the mantelpiece*) She's been very high-spirited all day. I know this mood of old. It usually meant that she was up to something.

(*Pause.* RUTH *shuts the door, and then comes across, below the sofa, to Charles*)

RUTH. You're sure she isn't here?

CHARLES. Quite sure.

RUTH. I want to talk to you.

CHARLES. Oh, God!

RUTH. I must—it's important.

(CHARLES *puts* RUTH *down into the* R *end of the sofa*)

CHARLES. You've behaved very well for the last few days, Ruth. You're not going to start making scenes again, are you?

RUTH. I resent that air of patronage, Charles. I have behaved well, as you call it, because there was nothing else to do, but I think it only fair to warn you that I offer no guarantee for the future. My patience is being stretched to its uttermost.

CHARLES (*crossing to the armchair and sitting*) As far as I can see the position is just as difficult for Elvira as it is for you—if not more so. The poor little thing comes back trustingly after all those years in the other world, and what is she faced with? Nothing but brawling and hostility!

RUTH. What did she expect?

CHARLES. Surely even an ectoplasmic manifestation has the right to expect a little of the milk of human kindness?

RUTH (*rising and going to the fireplace*) Milk of human fiddle-sticks!

CHARLES. That just doesn't make sense, dear.

RUTH (*coming to R of Charles and leaning over him*) Elvira is about as trusting as a puff-adder.

CHARLES. You're granite, Ruth—sheer unyielding granite.

RUTH. And a good deal more dangerous into the bargain.

CHARLES. Dangerous? I never heard anything so ridiculous. How could a poor lonely wistful little spirit like Elvira be dangerous?

RUTH. Quite easily—and she is. She's beginning to show her hand.

CHARLES. How do you mean—in what way?

RUTH. This is a fight, Charles—a bloody battle—a duel to the death between Elvira and me. Don't you realize that?

CHARLES. Melodramatic hysteria.

RUTH. It isn't melodramatic hysteria; it's true. Can't you see?

CHARLES. No, I can't. You're imagining things. Jealousy causes people to have the most curious delusions.

RUTH (*pausing*) I am making every effort not to lose my temper with you, Charles; but I must say you are making it increasingly difficult for me.

CHARLES. All this talk of battles and duels . . .

RUTH. She came here with one purpose and one purpose only —and if you can't see it you're a bigger fool than I thought you.

CHARLES. What purpose could she have had beyond a natural desire to see me again? After all, you must remember that she was extremely attached to me, poor child.

RUTH. Her purpose is perfectly obvious. It is to get you to herself for ever.

CHARLES. That's absurd. How could she?

RUTH. By killing you off, of course.

CHARLES. Killing me off? You're mad!

RUTH. Why do you suppose Edith fell down the stairs and nearly cracked her skull?

CHARLES. What's Edith got to do with it?

RUTH. Because the whole of the top stair was covered with axle grease. Cook discovered it afterwards.

CHARLES. You're making this up, Ruth.

RUTH. I'm not. I swear I'm not. Why do you suppose when you were lopping that dead branch off the pear tree that the ladder broke? Because it had been practically sawn through on both sides!

CHARLES (*rising*) But why should she want to kill me? I could understand her wanting to kill you, but why me?

RUTH. If you were dead it would be her final triumph over me. She'd have you with her for ever on her damned astral plane, and

I'd be left high and dry. She's probably planning a sort of spiritual re-marriage. I wouldn't put anything past her.

CHARLES (*really shocked*) Ruth!

RUTH. Don't you see now?

CHARLES (*crossing to the fireplace*) She couldn't be so sly, so wicked! She couldn't!

RUTH. Couldn't she just?

CHARLES. I grant you that as a character she was always rather light and irresponsible, but I would never have believed her capable of low cunning.

RUTH. Perhaps the spirit world has deteriorated her.

CHARLES. Oh, Ruth!

RUTH. For heaven's sake stop looking like a wounded spaniel and concentrate. This is serious.

CHARLES. What are we to do?

RUTH. You're not to let her know that we suspect a thing. Behave perfectly ordinarily, as though nothing had happened. I'm going to Madame Arcati immediately. I don't care how cross she is, she's got to help us—even if she can't get rid of Elvira she must know some technical method of rendering her harmless. If a trance is necessary she shall go into a trance if I have to beat her into it. I'll be back in half an hour. Tell Elvira I've got to see the vicar.

CHARLES. This is appalling . . .

RUTH. Never mind about that. Remember now, don't give yourself away by so much as a flick of an eyelid.

(*Light Cue No. 4. Act II, Scene 3*)

(ELVIRA *comes in from the garden. She comes to above the armchair*)

CHARLES. Look out!

RUTH. What?

CHARLES. I merely said it's a nice look out.

ELVIRA. What's a nice look out?

CHARLES. The weather, Elvira. The glass is going down and down and down. It's positively macabre.

ELVIRA. I find it difficult to believe that you and Ruth, at this particular moment, can't think of anything more interesting to talk about than the weather.

RUTH. I can't stand this any more. I really can't.

CHARLES. Ruth dear—please . . .

ELVIRA (*coming down* L, *by the gramophone*) Has she broken out again?

RUTH. What did she say?

CHARLES. She asked if you had broken out again.

RUTH (*coming across below the sofa and addressing Elvira up stage, with her back to Elvira*) How dare you talk like that, Elvira?

CHARLES. Now then, Ruth.

RUTH (*with dignity*) Charles and I were not talking about the weather, Elvira, as you so very shrewdly suspected. I should loathe you to think that we had any secrets from you.

(RUTH *is addressing Elvira up stage.* CHARLES *motions to Ruth that Elvira is behind her.* RUTH *turns and addresses her down stage.* ELVIRA *crosses below her to above the sofa*)

(*She repeats*) And so I will explain exactly what we were talking about. I was trying to persuade him *not* to drive you into Folkestone this evening. It will be bad for his arm and you can perfectly easily wait until tomorrow. However, as he seems to be determined to place your wishes before mine in everything, I have nothing further to say. (*She moves up* C *and turns*) I'm sure I hope you both enjoy yourselves.

(RUTH *goes out and slams the door*)

CHARLES. There now.

ELVIRA. Oh, Charles! Have you been beastly to her?

CHARLES. No. Ruth doesn't like being thwarted any more than you do.

ELVIRA. She's a woman of sterling character. It's a pity she's so ungiving.

CHARLES. As I told you before, I would rather not discuss Ruth with you. It makes me uncomfortable.

ELVIRA. I won't mention her again. Are you ready?

CHARLES. What for?

ELVIRA. To go to Folkestone, of course.

CHARLES. I want a glass of sherry first.

ELVIRA. I don't believe you want to take me at all.

CHARLES. Of course I want to take you, but I still think it would be more sensible to wait until tomorrow. It's a filthy night.

ELVIRA (*moving to and flinging herself into the armchair; crossly*) How familiar this is!

CHARLES. In what way familiar?

ELVIRA. All through our married life I only had to suggest something for you immediately to start hedging me off.

CHARLES. I'm not hedging you off, I merely said . . .

ELVIRA. All right—all right—we'll spend another cosy intimate evening at home with Ruth sewing away at that hideous table centre and snapping at us like a terrier.

CHARLES. Ruth is perfectly aware that the table centre is hideous. It happens to be a birthday present for her mother.

ELVIRA. It's no use trying to defend Ruth's taste to me. It's thoroughly artsy-craftsy and you know it.

CHARLES. It is not artsy-craftsy.

ELVIRA. She's ruined this room. Look at those curtains and that awful shawl on the piano.

CHARLES. Lady Mackinley sent it to us from Burma.

ELVIRA. Obviously because it had been sent to her from Birmingham.

CHARLES (*moving to R of Elvira*) If you don't behave yourself I shan't take you into Folkestone ever.

ELVIRA (*rising, coaxingly*) Please, Charles . . . don't be elderly and grand with me! Please let's go now!

CHARLES (*moving up to the drinks table*) Not until I've had my sherry.

ELVIRA. You are tiresome, darling. I've been waiting about for hours.

CHARLES. A few more minutes won't make any difference then. (*He pours himself out some sherry*)

ELVIRA (*petulantly, flinging herself into the chair again*) Oh, very well.

CHARLES. Besides, the car won't be back for half an hour at least.

ELVIRA (*sharply*) What do you mean?

CHARLES (*sipping his sherry nonchalantly*) Ruth's taken it. She had to go and see the vicar . . .

ELVIRA (*jumping up—in extreme agitation*) What!!

CHARLES. What on earth's the matter?

ELVIRA. You say *Ruth's* taken the car?

CHARLES. Yes. To go and see the vicar, but she won't be long.

ELVIRA (*going upstage c, wildly*) Oh, my God! Oh, my God!

CHARLES. Elvira!

ELVIRA. Stop her! You must stop her at once!

CHARLES. Why—what for?

ELVIRA (*jumping up and down*) Stop her! Go out and stop her immediately!

CHARLES. It's too late now—I heard her go a couple of minutes ago.

ELVIRA (*retreating backwards slowly towards the window.* CHARLES *comes to her*) Oh, oh, oh, oh!!

CHARLES. What are you going on like this for? What have you done?

ELVIRA (*frightened*) Done? I haven't done anything.

CHARLES. Elvira—you're lying.

ELVIRA (*backing away from him*) I'm not lying—what is there to lie about?

CHARLES. What are you in such a state for?

ELVIRA (*almost hysterical*) I'm not in a state—I don't know what you mean!

CHARLES. You've done something dreadful.

ELVIRA. Don't look at me like that, Charles! I haven't! I swear I haven't!

CHARLES (*stopping and taking a pace backwards away from her—striking his forehead*) My God! The car!

ELVIRA. No, Charles, no . . .

CHARLES. Ruth was right. You did want to kill me! You've done something to the car!

ELVIRA (*howling like a banshee*) Oh—oh—oh—oh!

CHARLES (*stepping towards her again*) What did you do? Answer me!

(*At this moment the telephone rings.* CHARLES *goes to the telephone upstage* R *on the drinks table*)

(*At the telephone*) Hallo—hallo! Yes, speaking . . . I see . . . the bridge at the bottom of the hill . . . thank you—no, I'll come at once.

(*He slowly puts back the receiver. As he does so the door bursts open.* ELVIRA *stands facing the door*)

ELVIRA (*obviously retreating from someone*) Well, of all the filthy low-down tricks . . . ! (*She runs across, below the sofa, shielding her head with her hands and screaming*) Ow—stop it—Ruth!—leave go . . . !

(ELVIRA *runs above the sofa to the door and out of the room, slamming the door. It opens again immediately and slams again.*

CHARLES, *standing still by the telephone, stares aghast*)

(*Light Cue No. 5. Act II, Scene 3*)

CURTAIN

ACT III

Scene 1

(Light Cue No. 1. Act III, Scene 1)

The time is evening a few days later. The doors are shut, the curtains are drawn. The windows, behind the curtains, are open.

CHARLES is standing before the fire drinking his after-dinner coffee. On both arms he wears a band of deep mourning. He finishes his coffee, puts the cup down on the mantelpiece, lights a cigarette and settles himself comfortably on the settee. He adjusts a reading-lamp, and with a sigh of well-being opens a novel and begins to read.

There is a ring at the front-door bell. With an exclamation of annoyance he puts down the book, gets up and goes into the hall. After a moment or so MADAME ARCATI comes in. CHARLES follows her and shuts the door. Madame Arcati is wearing the strange, rather barbaric evening clothes that she wore in Act I.

MADAME ARCATI. I hope you will not consider this an intrusion, Mr Condomine.

CHARLES. Not at all. Please sit down, won't you?

MADAME ARCATI. Thank you. *(She sits at the L end of the sofa)*

CHARLES (c) Would you like some coffee or a liqueur?

MADAME ARCATI. No, thank you. I had to come, Mr Condomine.

CHARLES *(politely)* Yes?

MADAME ARCATI. I felt a tremendous urge, like a rushing wind, and so I hopped on my bike and here I am.

CHARLES. It was very kind of you.

MADAME ARCATI. No, no, no. Not kind at all—it was my duty. I know it strongly.

CHARLES. Duty?

MADAME ARCATI. I reproach myself bitterly, you know.

CHARLES. Please don't. There is no necessity for that. *(He sits in the armchair)*

MADAME ARCATI. I allowed myself to get into a huff the other day with your late wife. I rode all the way home in the grip of temper, Mr Condomine. I have regretted it ever since.

CHARLES. My dear Madame Arcati——

MADAME ARCATI *(holding up her hand)* Please let me go on. Mine is the shame, mine is the blame. I shall never forgive myself. Had I not been so impetuous, had I listened to the cool voice of reason —so much might have been averted.

CHARLES. You told my wife distinctly that you were unable to help her. You were perfectly honest. Over and above the original unfortunate mistake I see no reason for you to reproach yourself.

MADAME ARCATI. I threw up the sponge! In a moment of crisis, I threw up the sponge instead of throwing down the gauntlet.

CHARLES. Whatever you threw, Madame Arcati, I very much fear nothing could have been done. It seems that circumstances have been a little too strong for all of us.

MADAME ARCATI. I cannot bring myself to admit defeat so easily. It is gall and wormwood to me. I could at least have concentrated—made an effort.

CHARLES. Never mind.

MADAME ARCATI. I do mind. I cannot help it. I mind with every fibre of my being. I have been thinking very carefully, I have also been reading up a good deal during the last few dreadful days. . . . I gather that we are alone?

CHARLES (*looking round*) My first wife is not in the room, she is lying down; the funeral exhausted her. I imagine that my second wife is with her; but of course I have no way of knowing for certain.

MADAME ARCATI. You have remarked no difference in the texture of your first wife since the accident?

CHARLES. No, she seems much as usual; a little under the weather, perhaps, a trifle low spirited, but that's all.

MADAME ARCATI. Well, that washes that out.

CHARLES. I'm afraid I don't understand.

MADAME ARCATI. Just a little theory I had. In the nineteenth century there was a pretty widespread belief that a ghost who had participated in the death of a human being disintegrated automatically.

CHARLES. How do you know that Elvira was in any way responsible for Ruth's death?

MADAME ARCATI. Elvira—such a pretty name—it has a definite lilt to it, hasn't it? (*She hums for a moment*) Elvira—El-vi-ra . . .

CHARLES (*rather agitated*) You haven't answered my question. How did you know?

MADAME ARCATI. It came to me last night, Mr Condomine. It came to me in a blinding flash. I had just finished my Ovaltine and turned the light out when I suddenly started up in bed with a loud cry—'Great Scott!' I said—'I've got it!' After that, I began to put two and two together. At three in the morning—with my brain fairly seething—I went to work on my crystal for a little. But it wasn't very satisfactory—cloudy, you know.

CHARLES (*uneasily*) I would be very much obliged if you would keep any theories you have regarding my wife's death to yourself, Madame Arcati. . . .

MADAME ARCATI. My one desire is to help you. I feel I have been dreadfully remiss over the whole affair. Not only remiss, but untidy.

CHARLES. I am afraid there is nothing whatever to be done.

MADAME ARCATI (*triumphantly*) But there is—there is! (*She produces a piece of paper from her bag and brandishes it*) I have found a formula—here it is! I copied it out of Edmondson's *Witchcraft and its Byways.*

CHARLES (*irritably*) What the hell are you talking about?

MADAME ARCATI (*rising*) Pluck up your heart, Mr Condomine! All is not lost!

CHARLES (*rising*) Now look here, Madame Arcati——

MADAME ARCATI. You are still anxious to dematerialize your first wife, I suppose?

CHARLES (*in a lower voice, with a cautious look towards the door*) Of course I am—I'm perfectly furious with her—but . . .

MADAME ARCATI. But what?

CHARLES. Well—she's been very upset for the last few days. You see, apart from me being angry with her, which she always hated even when she was alive, Ruth, my second wife, has hardly left her side a moment. You must see that she's been having a pretty bad time what with one thing and another.

MADAME ARCATI. Your delicacy of feeling does you credit; but I must say, if you will forgive my bluntness, that you are a damned fool, Mr Condomine.

CHARLES (*moving away to the L by the gramophone. Stiffly*) You are at liberty to think whatever you please.

MADAME ARCATI. Now, now, now—don't get on your high horse! There's no sense in that, is there? I have a formula here that I think will be able to get rid of her without hurting her feelings in the least. It's extremely simple and requires nothing more than complete concentration from you and a minor trance from me. I may even be able to manage it without lying down.

CHARLES. Honestly, I would rather——

(*At this moment the door opens and* ELVIRA *comes quickly into the room. She is obviously very upset*)

(*Light Cue No. 2. Act III, Scene 1*)

ELVIRA. Charles! (*She moves to above the sofa*)

CHARLES. What on earth's the matter?

ELVIRA (*seeing Madame Arcati*) Oh! What's she doing here?

CHARLES. She came to offer me her condolences.

ELVIRA (*moving above the sofa to the mantelpiece, then across, below Madame Arcati, and up to the piano*) They should have been congratulations.

CHARLES. Please don't say things like that, Elvira—it is in the worst possible taste. Madame Arcati, allow me to introduce my first wife, Elvira.

MADAME ARCATI. How do you do?

ELVIRA. What does she want, Charles? Send her away. (*She walks about the room*)

MADAME ARCATI. In what part of the room is she at the moment?

CHARLES. She's moving about rather rapidly. I'll tell you when and where she settles.

ELVIRA. She's the one who got me here in the first place, isn't she?

CHARLES. Yes.

ELVIRA. Well, please tell her to get me away again as soon as possible. I can't stand this house another minute.

CHARLES. Really, Elvira—I'm surprised at you.

ELVIRA (*nearly in tears*) I don't care how surprised you are. I want to go home. I'm sick of the whole thing.

CHARLES. Don't be childish, Elvira.

ELVIRA. I'm not being childish—I mean it.

MADAME ARCATI (*rising and moving to the fireplace—sniffing*) Very interesting—very interesting—I smell ectoplasm strongly!

ELVIRA. What a disgusting thing to say.

MADAME ARCATI (*up above the sofa to the R of Elvira, very excited*) Where is she now?

CHARLES. Here—close to me.

MADAME ARCATI (*mystically—stretching out her hands*) Are you happy, my dear?

ELVIRA (*stamping her foot*) Tell the silly old bitch to mind her own business!

MADAME ARCATI (*in a sing-song voice*) Was the journey difficult? Are you weary?

ELVIRA (*moving downstage L to the gramophone*) She's dotty.

CHARLES. Just a moment, Madame Arcati . . .

MADAME ARCATI (*with her eyes shut*) This is wonderful—wonderful——

ELVIRA. For God's sake tell her to go into the other room, Charles. I've got to talk to you.

CHARLES. Madame Arcati . . .

MADAME ARCATI. Just a moment. I almost have contact. I can sense the vibrations—this is magnificent . . .

CHARLES. Go on, Elvira—don't be a spoilsport—give her a bit of encouragement.

ELVIRA. If you'll promise to get her into the other room.

CHARLES. All right.

(ELVIRA *crosses below Madame Arcati to the R of her and blows gently into her ear*)

MADAME ARCATI (*jumping*) Yes, yes. Again! Again!

ELVIRA (*blowing in the other ear*) How's that?

MADAME ARCATI (*clasping and unclasping her hands in a frenzy of excitement*) This is first rate—it really is first rate! Absolutely stunning!

CHARLES. I'm so glad you're pleased.

ELVIRA. Please get rid of her. Ruth will be in in a minute.

CHARLES. Madame Arcati, would you think it most frightfully

rude if I asked you to go into the dining-room for a moment? My first wife wishes to speak to me alone.

MADAME ARCATI. Oh, must I? It's so lovely being actually in the room with her!

CHARLES. Only for a few minutes. I promise she'll be here when you come back.

MADAME ARCATI. Very well. Hand me my bag, will you? It's on the settee.

ELVIRA (*picking it up and handing it to her*) Here you are.

MADAME ARCATI (*taking it and blowing her a kiss*) Oh, you darling—you little darling!

(MADAME ARCATI, *humming ecstatically, goes out and into the dining-room and shuts the door*)

ELVIRA. How good is she really?

CHARLES. I don't know.

ELVIRA. Do you think she really could get me back again?

CHARLES. But my dear child . . .

ELVIRA. And don't call me your dear child. It's smug and super-cilious.

CHARLES. There's no need to be rude.

ELVIRA (*moving down stage to the mantelpiece and turning away*) The whole thing's been a failure—a miserable, dreary failure—and oh! what high hopes I started out with!

CHARLES (*moving towards Elvira*) You can't expect much sympathy from me, you know. I am perfectly aware that your highest hope was to murder me.

ELVIRA. Don't put it like that. It sounds so beastly.

CHARLES. It is beastly. It's one of the beastliest ideas I've ever heard.

ELVIRA. There was a time when you'd have welcomed the chance of being with me for ever and ever.

CHARLES. Your behaviour has shocked me immeasurably, Elvira. I had no idea you were so unscrupulous.

ELVIRA (*bursting into tears, and crossing below Charles to LC*) Oh, Charles . . .

CHARLES. Stop crying.

ELVIRA. They're only ghost tears. They don't mean anything really—but they're very painful.

CHARLES (*moving to the mantelpiece*) You've brought all this on yourself, you know.

ELVIRA (*coming to the back of the armchair*) That's right—rub it in. Anyhow, it was only because I loved you. The silliest thing I ever did in my whole life was to love you. You were always unworthy of me.

CHARLES. That remark comes perilously near impertinence, Elvira.

ELVIRA. I sat there, on the other side, just longing for you day after day. I did really. All through your affair with that brassy-looking woman in the South of France I went on loving you and thinking truly of you. Then you married Ruth and even then I forgave you and tried to understand because all the time I believed deep inside that you really loved me best . . . that's why I put myself down for a return visit and had to fill in all those forms and wait about in draughty passages for hours. If only you'd died before you met Ruth, everything might have been all right. She's absolutely ruined you. I hadn't been in the house a day before I realized that. Your books aren't a quarter as good as they used to be, either.

CHARLES (*incensed*) That is entirely untrue. Ruth helped me and encouraged me with my work, which is a damned sight more than you ever did.

ELVIRA. That's probably what's wrong with it.

CHARLES. All you ever thought of was going to parties and enjoying yourself.

ELVIRA. Why shouldn't I have fun? I died young, didn't I?

CHARLES. You needn't have died at all if you hadn't been idiotic enough to go out on the river with Guy Henderson and get soaked to the skin.

ELVIRA. So we're back at Guy Henderson again, are we?

CHARLES. You behaved abominably over Guy Henderson and it's no use pretending that you didn't.

ELVIRA (*sitting on the L arm of the armchair*) Guy adored me. And anyhow, he was very attractive.

CHARLES. You told me distinctly that he didn't attract you in the least.

ELVIRA. You'd have gone through the roof if I'd told you that he did.

CHARLES (*moving to below the sofa*) Did you have an affair with Guy Henderson?

ELVIRA. I would rather not discuss it, if you don't mind.

CHARLES. Answer me; did you or didn't you?

ELVIRA. Of course I didn't.

CHARLES. You let him kiss you though, didn't you?

ELVIRA. How could I stop him! He was bigger than I was.

CHARLES (*furiously*) And you swore to me——

ELVIRA. Of course I did. You were always making scenes over nothing at all.

CHARLES. Nothing at all!

ELVIRA. You never loved me a bit really. It was only your beastly vanity.

CHARLES. You seriously believe that it was only vanity that upset me when you went out in the punt with Guy Henderson?

ELVIRA. It was not a punt. It was a little launch.

CHARLES. I don't care if it was a three-masted schooner! You had no right to go!

ELVIRA. You seem to forget *why* I went! You seem to forget that you had spent the entire evening making sheep's eyes at that over-blown harridan with the false pearls.

CHARLES. A woman in Cynthia Cheviot's position would hardly wear false pearls.

ELVIRA. They were practically all she was wearing.

CHARLES. I am pained to observe that seven years in the echoing vaults of eternity have in no way impaired your native vulgarity.

ELVIRA. That was the remark of a pompous ass.

CHARLES (*moving upstage* R *to above the sofa, by the writing-table*) There is nothing to be gained by continuing this discussion.

ELVIRA. You always used to say that when you were thoroughly worsted.

CHARLES. On looking back on our married years, Elvira, I see now, with horrid clarity, that they were nothing but a mockery.

ELVIRA. You invite mockery, Charles. It's something to do with your personality, I think. A certain seedy grandeur!

CHARLES (*crossing towards Elvira below the sofa*) Once and for all, Elvira . . .

ELVIRA. You never suspected it, but I laughed at you steadily from the altar to the grave—all your ridiculous petty jealousies and your fussings and fumings——

CHARLES. You were feckless and irresponsible and morally un-stable. I realized that before we left Budleigh Salterton.

ELVIRA. Nobody but a monumental bore would have thought of having a honeymoon at Budleigh Salterton.

CHARLES. What's the matter with Budleigh Salterton?

ELVIRA. I was an eager young bride, Charles—I wanted glam-our and music and romance. All I got was potted palms, seven hours a day on a damp golf course, and a three-piece orchestra playing 'Merrie England'.

CHARLES. It's a pity you didn't tell me so at the time.

ELVIRA. I did, but you wouldn't listen. That's why I went out on the moors that day with Captain Bracegirdle. I was desperate.

CHARLES. You swore to me that you'd gone over to see your aunt in Exmouth!

ELVIRA. It was the moors.

CHARLES. With Captain Bracegirdle?

ELVIRA. With Captain Bracegirdle.

CHARLES (*furiously*) I might have known it! What a fool I was —what a blind fool! Did he make love to you?

ELVIRA (*sucking her finger and regarding it thoughtfully*) Of course.

CHARLES. Oh, Elvira!

ELVIRA. Only very discreetly—he was in the cavalry, you know.

CHARLES. Well, all I can say is that I'm well rid of you.

ELVIRA (*rising and moving to* L *below the piano*) Unfortunately you're not.

CHARLES. Oh yes, I am. You're dead and Ruth's dead. I shall sell this house, lock, stock and barrel, and go away.

ELVIRA. I shall follow you.

CHARLES. I shall go a long way away. I shall go to South America. You'll hate that; you were always such a bad traveller.

ELVIRA. That can't be helped. I shall have to follow you—you called me back.

CHARLES. I did *not* call you back!

ELVIRA. Well, somebody did—and it's hardly likely to have been Ruth.

CHARLES. Nothing in the world was further from my thoughts.

ELVIRA (*coming to the back of the armchair*) You were talking about me before dinner that evening.

CHARLES. I might just as easily have been talking about Joan of Arc, but that wouldn't necessarily mean that I wanted her to come and live with me.

ELVIRA. As a matter of fact, she's rather fun.

CHARLES. Stick to the point.

ELVIRA. When I think of what might have happened if I'd succeeded in getting you to the other world after all—it makes me shudder, it does honestly. It would be nothing but bickering and squabbling for ever and ever and ever. I swear I'll be better off with Ruth—at least she'll find her own set and not get in my way.

CHARLES. So I get in your way, do I?

ELVIRA. Only because I was idiotic enough to imagine that you loved me, and I sort of felt sorry for you.

CHARLES. I'm sick of these insults. Please go away.

ELVIRA. There's nothing I should like better. I've always believed in cutting my losses. That's why I died.

CHARLES. Of all the brazen sophistry . . .

ELVIRA. Call that old girl in again. Set her to work. I won't tolerate this any longer; I want to go home. (*She moves over to below the piano*)

(CHARLES *goes to* C *below sofa.* ELVIRA *starts to cry*)

CHARLES. For Heaven's sake don't snivel.

ELVIRA (*stamping her foot*) Call her in! She's got to get me out of this.

CHARLES (*going to the dining-room door*) I quite agree—and the sooner the better. (*He opens the door*) Madame Arcati, would you please come in now?

(MADAME ARCATI *comes in, followed by* CHARLES)

MADAME ARCATI (*eagerly*) Is the darling still here?

CHARLES (*grimly*) Yes, she is.

MADAME ARCATI. Where—tell me where?

CHARLES. Over by the piano, blowing her nose.

MADAME ARCATI (*approaching the piano above Elvira*) My dear—
oh, my dear . . . !

ELVIRA. Stop her fawning on me, Charles, or I shall break
something. (*She comes down* L)

(CHARLES *is above the* C *table.* MADAME ARCATI *is below the
piano*)

CHARLES. Elvira and I have discussed the whole situation.
Madame Arcati, and she wishes to go home immediately.

MADAME ARCATI. Home?

CHARLES. Wherever she came from.

MADAME ARCATI. You don't think she would like to stay a few
days longer—while I try to get things a little more organized?

ELVIRA. No—no! I want to go now.

MADAME ARCATI. I could come and be here with her; I could
bring my crystal.

ELVIRA. God forbid!

CHARLES. We are both agreed that she must go as soon as
possible. Please strain every nerve, Madame Arcati—make every
effort. You said something about a formula. What is it?

MADAME ARCATI (*reluctantly*) Well—if you insist——

CHARLES. I most emphatically do insist.

ELVIRA (*wailing*) Oh, Charles . . .

CHARLES. Shut up.

MADAME ARCATI. I can't guarantee anything, you know. I'll
do my best, but it may not work.

(MADAME ARCATI *moves the* C *table over to* LC. CHARLES *takes
the ashtray off it and puts it on the drinks table*)

CHARLES. What is the formula?

MADAME ARCATI. Nothing more than a little verse really. It
fell into disuse after the seventeenth century. I shall need some
pepper and salt.

CHARLES. There's some pepper and salt in the dining-room—
I'll get it.

(CHARLES *goes*)

MADAME ARCATI. We ought of course to have some shepherd's
wort and a frog or two, but I think I can manage without.

(MADAME ARCATI *talks to Elvira as though she were standing by
the piano.* CHARLES *comes back with the salt and pepper from the
dining-room*)

You won't be frightened, dear, will you? It's absolutely painless.

CHARLES (*showing the cruet*) Will this be enough?

MADAME ARCATI. Oh yes. I only need a little. Put it on the
table, please. Now then, let me see—— (*She fumbles in her bag for*

the paper and her glasses) Ah yes——— (*To Charles*) Sprinkle it, will
you—just a soupçon—there, right in the middle.

(CHARLES *does so*)

ELVIRA. This is going to be a flop. I can tell you that here and
now.

MADAME ARCATI. Now a few snapdragons out of that vase,
there's a good chap.

(CHARLES *brings the flowers from the vase on the drinks table and
comes to* R *of the séance table.* MADAME ARCATI *is above the table.*
ELVIRA *is by the gramophone*)

CHARLES. Here you are.

ELVIRA. Merlin does all this sort of thing at parties and bores
us all stiff with it.

MADAME ARCATI. Now then, the gramophone. In the old days,
of course, they used a zither or reed pipes. We'd better have the
same record we had before, I think.

ELVIRA. I'll get it.

(ELVIRA *gets the record and gives it to* MADAME ARCATI, *then
crosses to the fireplace*)

CHARLES. Whatever you think best, Madame Arcati.

MADAME ARCATI (*watching, fascinated*) Oh, if only that Mr Ems-
worth of the Psychical Research could see this! He'd have a fit, he
would really!

(MADAME ARCATI *puts the record on the gramophone; addressing*
ELVIRA *downstage* L. CHARLES *sits above the table on the piano-stool*)

Don't start it yet, dear. Now then. Sit down, please, Mr Condomine; rest your hands on the table, but don't put your fingers in
the pepper. I shall turn out the lights myself. Oh, shucks, I'd
nearly forgotten! (*She goes to the table and makes designs in the
sprinkled pepper and salt with her finger*) One triangle—(*she consults
the paper*) one half-circle and one little dot. There!

ELVIRA. This is waste of time. She's a complete fake.

CHARLES. Anything's worth trying.

ELVIRA. I'm as eager for it to succeed as you are. Don't make
any mistake about that. But I'll lay you ten to one it's a dead
failure.

MADAME ARCATI. Now, if your wife would be kind enough to
lie down on the sofa.

CHARLES. Go on, Elvira.

ELVIRA (*lying down*) This is sheer nonsense. Don't blame me if
I get the giggles.

CHARLES. Concentrate—think of nothing.

MADAME ARCATI (*crosses to Elvira on the sofa. She faces Elvira's
feet instead of her head*) That's right—quite right—hands at the

sides—legs extended—breathe steadily—one, two—one, two—
one, two. Is she comfortable?

CHARLES. Are you comfortable, Elvira?

ELVIRA. No.

CHARLES. She's quite comfortable.

MADAME ARCATI. I shall join you in a moment, Mr Condomine. I may have to go into a slight trance, but if I do, pay no
attention. Now first the music, and away we go! (*She crosses to the
gramophone*)

(MADAME ARCATI *turns on the gramophone and stands quite still
by the side of it with her hands behind her head for a little. Then
suddenly, with great swiftness, she runs to the door and switches out the
lights*)

(*Light Cue No. 3. Act III, Scene 1*)

(*Her form can be dimly discerned moving about in the darkness.*
CHARLES *gives a loud sneeze*)

ELVIRA (*giggling*) Oh dear—it's the pepper.

CHARLES. Damm!

MADAME ARCATI. Hold on to yourself—concentrate! (*She recites
in a sing-song voice*)

> Ghostly spectre—ghoul or fiend,
> Never more be thou convened;
> Shepherd's Wort and Holy Rite
> Banish thee into the night.

ELVIRA. What a disagreeable little verse!

CHARLES. Be quiet, Elvira!

MADAME ARCATI (*pulling up the chair downstage L and sitting opposite Charles*) Sssh! (*There is silence*) Is there anyone there? . . . Is
there anyone there? . . . One rap for yes—two raps for no . . .
Is there anyone there? . . . (*The table gives a loud bump*) Aha—good
stuff! Is that you, Daphne? . . . (*The table gives another bump*) I'm
sorry to bother you, dear, but Mrs Condomine wants to return.
(*The table bumps several times very quickly*) Now then, Daphne . . .
Did you hear what I said? (*After a pause the table gives one bump*)
Can you help us? . . . (*There is another pause, then the table begins to
bump violently without stopping*) Hold tight, Mr Condomine—it's
trying to break away—oh—oh—oh——! (*The table falls over with
a crash. She falls off the chair and pulls over the table on to her*)

CHARLES. What's the matter, Madame Arcati? Are you hurt?

MADAME ARCATI (*wailing*) Oh—oh—oh——!

(CHARLES *rushes to the door and turns on the lights*)

(*Light Cue No. 4. Act III, Scene 1*)

(*He then goes back to Madame Arcati and kneels above her*)

CHARLES. What on earth's happening?

(Mᴀᴅᴀᴍᴇ Aʀᴄᴀᴛɪ *is lying on the floor with the table upside down on her back.* Cʜᴀʀʟᴇs *hurriedly lifts it off*)

(*Shaking her*) Are you hurt, Madame Arcati?

(Eʟᴠɪʀᴀ *rises and comes and looks at* Mᴀᴅᴀᴍᴇ Aʀᴄᴀᴛɪ; *then she crosses back to the fireplace above the sofa*)

Eʟᴠɪʀᴀ (*as she moves*) She's in one of her damned trances again, and I'm here as much as ever I was.
Cʜᴀʀʟᴇs (*shaking Madame Arcati*) For God's sake wake up!
Eʟᴠɪʀᴀ. Leave her alone. She's having the whale of a time.
Mᴀᴅᴀᴍᴇ Aʀᴄᴀᴛɪ (*moaning*) Oh—oh—oh——!
Eʟᴠɪʀᴀ. If I ever do get back I'll strangle that bloody little Daphne.
Mᴀᴅᴀᴍᴇ Aʀᴄᴀᴛɪ (*sitting up suddenly*) What happened?
Cʜᴀʀʟᴇs. Nothing—nothing at all.

(Mᴀᴅᴀᴍᴇ Aʀᴄᴀᴛɪ *rises.* Cʜᴀʀʟᴇs *rises and picks up the table*)

Mᴀᴅᴀᴍᴇ Aʀᴄᴀᴛɪ (*dusting herself*) Oh yes, it did. I know something happened.
Cʜᴀʀʟᴇs. You fell over. That's all that happened.
Mᴀᴅᴀᴍᴇ Aʀᴄᴀᴛɪ. Is she still here?
Cʜᴀʀʟᴇs. Of course she is.
Mᴀᴅᴀᴍᴇ Aʀᴄᴀᴛɪ. Something must have gone wrong.
Eʟᴠɪʀᴀ. Make her do it properly. I'm sick of being messed about like this!

(Cʜᴀʀʟᴇs *moves to above the sofa.* Mᴀᴅᴀᴍᴇ Aʀᴄᴀᴛɪ *moves up to* ᴄ *by the door*)

Cʜᴀʀʟᴇs. Be quiet! She's doing her best.
Mᴀᴅᴀᴍᴇ Aʀᴄᴀᴛɪ. Something happened. I sensed it in my trance—I felt it—it shivered through me.

(*Suddenly the window curtains blow out almost straight and* Rᴜᴛʜ *walks into the room. She is still wearing the brightly coloured clothes in which we last saw her, but now they are entirely grey. So is her hair and skin*)

Rᴜᴛʜ (*entering from the windows and going straight towards Charles,* ᴄ) Once and for all, Charles—what the hell does this mean?

(*Light Cue No. 5. Act III, Scene 1*)

The Lɪɢʜᴛs *fade*

SCENE 2

(*Light Cue No. 1. Act III, Scene 2*)

When the LIGHTS go up again several hours have elapsed. The doors are shut, the curtains are drawn. The windows are open, behind the curtains. The whole room is in slight disarray. There are birch branches and evergreens laid on the floor in front of the doors and crossed birch branches pinned rather untidily on to the curtains. The furniture has been moved about a bit. On the bridge table there is a pile of playing cards, Madame Arcati's crystal and a ouija board. Also a plate of sandwiches and two empty beer-mugs.

MADAME ARCATI *is asleep on the sofa, her head to the fireplace.* RUTH *is leaning on the mantelpiece.* CHARLES *is sitting on the back of the sofa.* ELVIRA *is sitting on the piano-stool above the séance table.*

RUTH. Well—we've done all we can. I must say I couldn't be more exhausted.

ELVIRA. It will be daylight soon.

(*The clock strikes five, very slowly*)

RUTH. That clock's always irritated me. It strikes far too slowly.

CHARLES. It was a wedding present from Uncle Walter.

RUTH. Whose Uncle Walter?

CHARLES. Elvira's.

RUTH. Well, all I can say is he might have chosen something a little more decorative.

ELVIRA. If that really were all you could say, Ruth, I'm sure it would be a great comfort to us all.

RUTH (*grandly*) You can be as rude as you like, Elvira. I don't mind a bit. As a matter of fact, I should be extremely surprised if you weren't.

ELVIRA (*truculently*) Why?

RUTH. The reply to that is really too obvious.

CHARLES. I wish you two would stop bickering for one minute.

RUTH. This is quite definitely one of the most frustrating nights I have ever spent.

ELVIRA. The reply to that is pretty obvious, too.

RUTH. I'm sure I don't know what you mean.

ELVIRA. Skip it!

RUTH (*crossing to the R of Elvira, below the sofa and above the arm-chair*) Now listen to me, Elvira. If you and I have got to stay together indefinitely in this house, and it looks unpleasantly likely, we had better come to some sort of an arrangement.

ELVIRA. What sort of an arrangement?

CHARLES (*moving above the sofa to the fireplace*) You're *not* going to stay indefinitely in this house.

RUTH. With you, then—we shall have to be with you.

CHARLES. I don't see why. Why don't you take a cottage some-where?

RUTH. You called us back.

CHARLES. I've already explained until I'm black in the face that I did nothing of the sort.

RUTH. Madame Arcati said you did.

CHARLES. Madame Arcati's a muddling old fool.

ELVIRA. I could have told you that in the first place.

RUTH. I think you're behaving very shabbily, Charles.

CHARLES. I don't see what I've done.

RUTH. We all agreed that as Elvira and I are dead that it would be both right and proper for us to dematerialize again as soon as possible. (*She sits on the L arm of the armchair*) That I admit. We have allowed ourselves to be subjected to the most humiliating hocus-pocus for hours and hours without complaining . . .

CHARLES (*sitting on the L arm of the sofa*) Without complaining?

RUTH. We've stood up. We've lain down. We've concentrated. We've sat interminably while that tiresome old woman recited extremely unflattering verses at us. We've endured five séances. We've watched her fling herself in and out of trances until we're dizzy, and at the end of it all we find ourselves exactly where we were at the beginning.

CHARLES. Well, it's not my fault.

RUTH. Be that as it may, the least you could do is to admit failure gracefully and try to make the best of it. Your manners are boorish to a degree.

CHARLES (*rising*) I'm just as exhausted as you are. I've had to do all the damned table tapping, remember.

RUTH. If she can't get us back she can't, and that's that. We shall have to think of something else.

CHARLES (*crossing to the mantelpiece*) She *must* get you back. Anything else is unthinkable.

ELVIRA. There's gratitude for you!

CHARLES. Gratitude?

ELVIRA. Yes, for all the years we've both devoted to you. You ought to be ashamed.

CHARLES. What about all the years I've devoted to you?

ELVIRA. Nonsense. We've waited on you hand and foot—haven't we, Ruth? You're exceedingly selfish, and always were.

CHARLES. In that case I fail to see why you were both so anxious to get back to me.

RUTH. You called us back. And you've done nothing but try to get rid of us ever since we came—hasn't he, Elvira?

ELVIRA. He certainly has.

RUTH. And now, owing to your idiotic inefficiency, we find ourselves in the most mortifying position. We're neither fish, flesh, nor fowl, nor whatever it is.

ELVIRA. Good red herring.

RUTH. It can't be.

CHARLES. Well, why don't you do something about it? Why

don't you go back on your own? (*He comes between Ruth and Elvira*)

RUTH. We can't—you know perfectly well we can't.

CHARLES. Isn't there anybody on the Other Side who can help?

RUTH. How do I know? I've only been there a few days . . . Ask Elvira.

ELVIRA. I've already told you that it's no good. If we got Cagliostro, Mesmer, Merlin, Gil de Retz and the Black Douglas in a row they couldn't do a thing. The impetus has got to come from here . . . Perhaps Charles doesn't want us to go quite enough.

CHARLES (*moving away quickly to* R *above the sofa*) I certainly do.

ELVIRA. Well, you must have a very weak will, then. I always suspected it.

RUTH. It's no use arguing any more. Wake up, Madame Arcati.

ELVIRA. Oh, not another séance—please, not another séance!

CHARLES (*bending over the back of the sofa; loudly*) Please wake up, Madame Arcati.

RUTH. Shake her.

CHARLES. It might upset her.

RUTH. I don't care if it kills her.

CHARLES. Please wake up, Madame Arcati.

MADAME ARCATI (*waking*) What time is it?

CHARLES. Ten past five!

MADAME ARCATI. What time did I go off? (*She sits up*)

CHARLES. Over an hour ago.

MADAME ARCATI (*reaching for her bag*) Curious . . very curious. Forgive me for a moment, I must make a note of that for my diary. (*She takes a book out of her bag and scribbles in it*) Are they still here?

CHARLES. Yes.

MADAME ARCATI. How disappointing.

(CHARLES *is at the* L *end of the sofa,* RUTH *in the armchair*)

CHARLES. Have you any suggestions?

MADAME ARCATI (*rising briskly*) We mustn't give up hope. Chin up—never give in—that's my motto.

RUTH. This schoolgirl phraseology's driving me mad.

MADAME ARCATI (*coming a pace down*) Now then . . .

CHARLES. Now then what?

MADAME ARCATI. What do you say we have another séance and really put our shoulders to the wheel? Make it a real rouser?

ELVIRA. For God's sake not another séance!

MADAME ARCATI. I might be able to materialize a trumpet if I tried hard enough—better than nothing, you know. I feel as fit as a fiddle after my rest.

ELVIRA. I don't care if she materializes a whole symphony orchestra. I implore you not to let her have another séance.

C*

CHARLES. Don't you think, Madame Arcati, that perhaps we've had enough séances? After all, they haven't achieved much, have they?

MADAME ARCATI. Rome wasn't built in a day, you know.

CHARLES. I know it wasn't, but . . .

MADAME ARCATI. Well then—cheer up—away with melancholy.

CHARLES. Now listen, Madame Arcati . . . before you go off into any further trances I really think we ought to discuss the situation a little.

MADAME ARCATI. Good! An excellent idea! And while we're doing it I shall have another of these delicious sandwiches—I'm as hungry as a hunter. (*She goes to the table and gets a sandwich; then moves to the fireplace*)

CHARLES. Would you like some more beer?

MADAME ARCATI. No, thank you. Better not.

CHARLES. Very well; I think I'll have a small whisky and soda.

MADAME ARCATI. Make it a double and enjoy yourself.

(CHARLES *goes to the drinks table and mixes himself a whisky and soda*)

RUTH. One day I intend to give myself the pleasure of telling Madame Arcati exactly what I think of her.

CHARLES. She's been doing her best.

MADAME ARCATI. Are the girls getting despondent?

CHARLES. I'm afraid they are, rather.

MADAME ARCATI. We'll win through yet. Don't be downhearted! (*She sits on the sofa*)

RUTH. If we're not very careful she'll materialize a hockey team.

MADAME ARCATI. Now then, Mr Condomine—the discussion. Fire away.

CHARLES (*coming to and sitting on the pouffe downstage* R) Well, my wives and I have been talking it over and they are both absolutely convinced that I somehow or other called them back.

MADAME ARCATI. Very natural.

CHARLES. I am convinced that I did not.

MADAME ARCATI. Love is a strong psychic force, Mr Condomine. It can work untold miracles. A true love call can encompass the universe.

CHARLES (*hastily*) I'm sure it can, but I must confess to you frankly that although my affection for both Elvira and Ruth is of the warmest, I cannot truthfully feel that it would come under the heading that you describe.

ELVIRA. I should just think not, indeed.

MADAME ARCATI. You may not know your own strength, Mr Condomine.

CHARLES (*firmly*) I did *not* call them back—either consciously or sub-consciously.

MADAME ARCATI. But Mr Condomine——

CHARLES. That is my final word on the subject.

MADAME ARCATI. Neither of them could have appeared unless there had been somebody—a psychic subject—in the house, who wished for them——

CHARLES. Well, it wasn't me.

ELVIRA. Perhaps it was Doctor Bradman. I never knew he cared.

MADAME ARCATI. Are you sure? Are you really sure?

CHARLES. Absolutely positive.

MADAME ARCATI (*throwing the sandwich over her head and rising*) Great Scott, I believe I've been barking up the wrong tree!

CHARLES. How do you mean?

MADAME ARCATI. The Sudbury case!

CHARLES. I don't understand.

MADAME ARCATI. There's no reason why you should; it was before your day. I wonder—oh, I wonder . . . (*She crosses to L up stage*)

CHARLES. What was the Sudbury case? I wish you'd explain.

MADAME ARCATI (*above Ruth in the armchair*) It was the case that made me famous, Mr Condomine. It was what you might describe in theatrical parlance as my first smash hit! I had letters from all over the world about it, especially India.

CHARLES. What did you do?

MADAME ARCATI (*sitting on the L arm of the armchair and leaning over Ruth*) I dematerialized old Lady Sudbury after she'd been firmly entrenched in the private chapel for over seventeen years.

CHARLES. How? Can you remember how?

MADAME ARCATI. Chance—a fluke! I happened on it by the merest coincidence.

CHARLES. What fluke? What was it?

MADAME ARCATI. Wait! All in good time. (*She begins to walk about the room*) Now let me see—who was in the house during our first séance? (*She moves to the writing-desk*)

CHARLES. Only the Bradmans, Ruth and me and yourself.

MADAME ARCATI. Ah yes—yes, to be sure! But the Bradmans weren't here last night, were they?

CHARLES. No.

MADAME ARCATI. Quickly—my crystal——

CHARLES (*moving below the sofa and getting the crystal from the table L and giving it to Madame Arcati above the sofa*) Here . . .

MADAME ARCATI (*shaking it crossly*) Damn the thing, it gives me the pip. It's cloudy again! (*She looks again*) Ah! That's better—it's there again—it's there again! I'm beginning to understand.

CHARLES. I wish I was. What's there again?

MADAME ARCATI. A bandage . . . a white bandage—hold on to a white bandage . . .

CHARLES. I haven't got a white bandage.

MADAME ARCATI. Sssh! (*She crosses to the séance-table and puts the crystal down. She stands silently for a moment*)

ELVIRA. She's too good, you know. She ought to be in a circus.

(MADAME ARCATI *runs across and leaps on to the pouffe. Then she raises her arms slowly—begins to intone*)

MADAME ARCATI.

     Be you in nook or cranny, answer me,
     Be you in still-room or closet, answer me,
     Be you behind the panel, above the stairs,
     Beneath the eaves—waking or sleeping,
     Answer me!

(*She jumps down*) That ought to do it or I'm a Dutchman. (*She moves to the middle of the room*)

CHARLES. Do what?

MADAME ARCATI. Hush—wait——!

(MADAME ARCATI *crosses to the window and picks up a bunch of garlic and crosses to the writing-desk, making cabalistic signs. She picks up one of the birch branches and waves it solemnly to and fro*)

RUTH (*rising and moving to the gramophone*) For God's sake don't let her throw any more of that garlic about. It nearly made me sick last time.

CHARLES. Would you like the gramophone on or the lights out or anything?

MADAME ARCATI. No, no—it's near—it's very near——

ELVIRA (*rising and coming L to the gramophone, above Ruth*) If it's a ghost, I shall scream.

RUTH. I hope it's nobody we know. I shall feel so silly.

(*Suddenly the door opens and* EDITH *comes into the room. She is wearing a pink flannel dressing-gown and bedroom slippers. Her head is bandaged*)

EDITH. Did you ring, sir?

MADAME ARCATI. The bandage! The white bandage!

CHARLES. No, Edith.

EDITH. I'm sorry, sir—I could have sworn I heard the bell—or somebody calling. I was asleep—I don't rightly know which it was.

MADAME ARCATI. Come here, child.

EDITH. Oh! (*She looks anxiously at Charles*)

CHARLES (*moving up to L of* EDITH, *who comes* C, L *of Madame Arcati*) Go on! Go to Madame Arcati—it's quite all right!

MADAME ARCATI. Whom do you see in this room, child?

EDITH. Oh dear . . .

MADAME ARCATI. Answer, please.

EDITH (*falteringly*) You, Madame—— (*She stops*)

MADAME ARCATI. Go on.

EDITH. The master.

MADAME ARCATI. Anyone else?

EDITH. Oh, no, Madame . . .

MADAME ARCATI (*inflexibly*) Look again.

EDITH (*imploringly, to Charles*) I don't understand, sir—I——

MADAME ARCATI. Come, child—don't beat about the bush. Look again.

(ELVIRA *moves across to the fireplace below the sofa, almost as though she were being pulled.* RUTH *follows. Both stand at the fire.* ELVIRA *up stage.* EDITH *follows them with her eyes*)

RUTH. Do concentrate, Elvira, and keep still.

ELVIRA. I can't . . .

MADAME ARCATI. Do you see anyone else now?

EDITH (*slyly*) Oh, no, Madame.

MADAME ARCATI. She's lying.

EDITH. Oh, Madame!

MADAME ARCATI. They always do.

CHARLES. They?

MADAME ARCATI (*sharply*) Where are they now?

EDITH. By the fireplace—oh!

CHARLES. She can see them—do you mean she can see them?

MADAME ARCATI. Probably not very clearly—but enough——

EDITH (*bursting into tears*) Let me go! I haven't done nothing nor seen nobody! Let me go back to bed!

MADAME ARCATI. Give her a sandwich.

(CHARLES *goes to the table and gets a sandwich for Edith*)

EDITH (*drawing away*) I don't want a sandwich. I want to get back to bed!

CHARLES (*handing Edith the plate*) Here, Edith.

MADAME ARCATI. Nonsense! A big healthy girl like you saying no to a delicious sandwich! I never heard of such a thing! Sit down!

(MADAME ARCATI *brings* EDITH *to the* R *arm of the chair.* CHARLES *is* L *of her.* MADAME ARCATI *is in front of her*)

EDITH (*to Charles*) Please, sir, I . . .

CHARLES. Please do as Madame Arcati says, Edith.

EDITH (*sitting down on the arm of the armchair and sniffing*) I haven't done nothing wrong.

CHARLES. It's all right—nobody said you had.

RUTH. If she's been the cause of all this unpleasantness I'll give her a week's notice tomorrow.

ELVIRA. You may not be here tomorrow.

MADAME ARCATI. Look at me, Edith.

(EDITH *obediently does so*)

Cuckoo—cuckoo—cuckoo——!

EDITH (*jumping*) Oh dear—what's the matter with her? Is she barmy?

MADAME ARCATI. Here, Edith—this is my finger. Look! (*She waggles it*) Have you ever seen such a long, long, long finger? Look, now it's on the right—now it's on the left—backwards and forwards it goes—see—very quietly backwards and forwards— tic-toc—tic-toc—tic-toc.

ELVIRA. The mouse ran up the clock.

RUTH. Be quiet, you'll ruin everything.

(MADAME ARCATI *whistles a little tune close to Edith's face. Then she snaps her fingers. EDITH looks stolidly in front of her without flinching. MADAME ARCATI stands back*)

MADAME ARCATI. Well—so far so good—she's off all right.

CHARLES. Off?

MADAME ARCATI. She's a Natural. Just the same as the Sudbury case, it really is the most amusing coincidence. Now then—would you ask your wives to stand close together, please?

CHARLES. Where? (*He drops downstage* L)

MADAME ARCATI. Over there by you.

CHARLES. Elvira! Ruth!

(RUTH *and* ELVIRA *move slowly behind the sofa to the french windows during the following sentences*)

RUTH. I resent being ordered about like this.

ELVIRA. I don't like this at all. I don't like any of it. I feel peculiar.

CHARLES. I'm afraid I must insist.

ELVIRA. It would serve you right if we flatly refused to do anything at all.

MADAME ARCATI. Are you sorry for having been so mischievous, Edith?

EDITH (*cheerfully*) Oh, yes, Madame!

MADAME ARCATI. You know what you have to do now, don't you, Edith?

EDITH. Oh, yes, Madame.

(CHARLES *moves across to the fireplace*)

RUTH. I believe it's going to work, whatever it is . . . Oh, Charles!

CHARLES. Sssh!

RUTH. This is good-bye, Charles.

ELVIRA. Tell her to stop for a minute. There's something I want to say before I go.

CHARLES. You should have thought of that before. It's too late now.

ELVIRA. Of all the mean, ungracious——
RUTH. Charles, listen a moment——
MADAME ARCATI (*in a shrill voice*) Lights!

(MADAME ARCATI *rushes to the door and switches off the lights*)

(*Light Cue No. 2. Act III, Scene 2*)

(*In the dark* EDITH *is singing 'Always' in a very high Cockney voice.*
ELVIRA *and* RUTH *both go through the window*)

ELVIRA (*in the dark*) I saw Captain Bracegirdle again, Charles—several times—I went to the Four Hundred with him twice when you were in Nottingham, and I must say I couldn't have enjoyed it more.

RUTH. Don't think you're getting rid of us quite so easily, my dear—you may not be able to see us, but we shall be here all right—I consider that you have behaved atrociously over the whole miserable business, and I should like to say here and now . . .

(*Her voice fades into a whisper and then disappears altogether*)

MADAME ARCATI (*exultantly*) Splendid—hurrah! We've done it! That's quite enough singing for the moment, Edith.
CHARLES (*after a pause*) Shall I put on the lights?
MADAME ARCATI. No, I will. (*She switches on the lights*)

(*Light Cue No. 3. Act III, Scene 2*)

(CHARLES *crosses to the window and pulls the curtains*)

(*Light Cue No. 4. Act III, Scene 2*)

(*Daylight floods into the room.* RUTH *and* ELVIRA *have disappeared.* EDITH *is sitting still on the chair*)

CHARLES. They've gone! They've really gone!
MADAME ARCATI. Yes—I think we've really pulled it off this time. (*She moves to below the sofa*)
CHARLES. You'd better wake her up, hadn't you? She might bring them back again.
MADAME ARCATI (*going to the* L *of Edith; clapping her hands in Edith's face*) Wake up, child!
EDITH (*jumping up from the chair*) Good 'Eavens! Where am I?
CHARLES. It's all right, Edith. You can go back to bed now.
EDITH. Why, it's morning.
CHARLES. Yes, I know it is.
EDITH. But I *was* in bed! How did I get down 'ere?
CHARLES. I rang, Edith. I rang the bell and you answered it; didn't I, Madame Arcati?

EDITH. Did I drop off? Do you think it's my concussion again? Oh dear!

CHARLES. Off you go, Edith, and thank you very much. (*He presses a pound note into her hands*) Thank you very much indeed.

EDITH. Oh, sir, whatever for? (*She looks at him in sudden horror*) Oh, sir!!

(EDITH *bolts from the room*)

CHARLES (*surprised*) What on earth did she mean by that?

MADAME ARCATI (*sitting in the middle of the sofa*) Golly, what a night! I'm ready to drop in my tracks.

CHARLES. Would you like to stay here? There's the spare room, you know.

MADAME ARCATI. No, thank you. Each to his own nest. I'll pedal home in a jiffy, it's only seven miles. (*She rises and faces Charles*)

CHARLES. I'm deeply grateful to you, Madame Arcati. I don't know what arrangements you generally make, but I trust you will send in your account in due course.

MADAME ARCATI. Good heavens, Mr Condomine—it was a pleasure! I wouldn't dream of such a thing.

CHARLES. But really I feel that all those trances . . .

MADAME ARCATI. I enjoy them, Mr Condomine, thoroughly. I always have, since a child.

CHARLES. Perhaps you'd give me the pleasure of lunching with me one day soon?

MADAME ARCATI. When you come back, I should be delighted.

CHARLES. Come back?

(MADAME ARCATI *crosses to the table* LC *and kneels to pick up the cards from the floor.* CHARLES *is* C)

MADAME ARCATI (*lowering her voice*) Take my advice, Mr Condomine, and go away immediately.

CHARLES. But Madame Arcati! You don't mean that . . . ?

MADAME ARCATI. This must be an unhappy house for you. There must be memories both grave and gay in every corner of it—also—— (*She pauses*)

CHARLES. Also what?

MADAME ARCATI (*thinking better of it*) There are more things in heaven and earth, Mr Condomine. (*She places her finger to her lips*) Just go. Pack your traps and go as soon as possible. (*She rises and goes to Charles*)

CHARLES (*also in lowered tones*) Do you mean that they may still be here?

MADAME ARCATI (*nodding and nonchalantly whistling a little tune*) *Quien sabe*, as the Spanish say.

(MADAME ARCATI *goes to the table and collects her crystal, cards and ouija board*)

CHARLES (*looking furtively round the room*) I wonder—I wonder. I'll follow your advice, Madame Arcati. Thank you again.

MADAME ARCATI. Well, goodbye, Mr Condomine. It's been fascinating—from first to last—fascinating. Do you mind if I take just one more sandwich to munch on my way home? (*She gets a sandwich from the table*)

CHARLES. By all means.

(MADAME ARCATI *goes to the door.* CHARLES *follows her to see her safely out*)

MADAME ARCATI (*as they go*) Don't trouble—I can find my way. Cheerio once more, and Good Hunting!

(CHARLES *watches her into the hall and then comes back into the room*)

CHARLES (*starting to speak at the door. Softly*) Ruth!—Elvira!—are you there? (*A pause*) Ruth!—Elvira!—I know damn well you're there. (*Another pause*) I just want to tell you that I'm going away, so there's no point in your hanging about any longer—I'm going a long way away—somewhere where I don't believe you'll be able to follow me—in spite of what Elvira said I don't think spirits can travel over water. Is that quite clear, my darlings? You said in one of your more acid moments, Ruth, that I had been hag-ridden all my life! How right you were! But now I'm free, Ruth dear, not only of Mother and Elvira and Mrs Winthrop-Llewellyn, but free of you too, and I should like to take this fare-well opportunity of saying I'm enjoying it immensely——

(*The vase on the mantelpiece falls on to the hearth-stone and smashes*)

Aha!—I thought so—you were very silly, Elvira, to imagine that I didn't know all about you and Captain Bracegirdle. I did. But what you didn't know was that I was extremely attached to Paula Westlake at the time!

(*The picture above the piano crashes to the ground*)

I was reasonably faithful to you, Ruth, but I doubt if it would have lasted much longer. You were becoming increasingly dom-ineering, you know, and there's nothing more off-putting than that, is there?

(*The clock strikes sixteen very quickly*)

Good-bye for the moment, my dears! I expect we are bound to meet again one day, but until we do I'm going to enjoy myself as I've never enjoyed myself before.

(*A sofa cushion is thrown into the air towards Charles from behind the sofa*)

You can break up the house as much as you like—I'm leaving it anyhow. Think kindly of me, and send out good thoughts.

(*The curtains are pulled up and down, the gramophone lid opens and shuts.*

The overmantel begins to shake and tremble as though someone were tugging at it)

Nice work, Ruth—get Elvira to help you . . . persevere!

(*A figure from above the* R *bookshelves falls off on to the floor*)

Good-bye again! Parting is such *sweet* sorrow!

(*A vase from the bookshelves up stage falls. The window curtains fall. The gramophone starts playing 'Always' very quickly and loudly.*

CHARLES *goes out of the room just as the overmantel crashes to the floor and the curtain-pole comes tumbling down*)

CURTAIN

PROPERTY PLOT USED AT THE PICCADILLY THEATRE, LONDON

ACT I, Scene 1

On Stage
  On small table down R—*Top rung*—White vase of tall daisies. Ashtray
    Lower rung—Red fruit dish
  On mantelpiece—2 statuettes (for breaking)
    2 cups and saucers
    Clock (centre)
    Cigarette-box and matches
    2 small ornaments
  On desk upstage R—Silver inkstand
    Blotter
    Leather writing-pad
    Book
    Desk lamp (green shade)
    Small white china bowl
    Staffordshire figure
  On table upstage RC—Telephone (white)
    Tall vase of red peonies
    Small glass ashtray and matches
  On piano upstage L—Shawl draped over piano
    Cigarette-box and matches
    Standing mirror
    Lamp
    Small glass bowl of mixed flowers
  On flat above piano—Picture, to fall in Act III
  On small white table—Green cigarette-box
  On small table C—Silver cigarette-box
    Large square green ashtray
  Top of bookshelves at back—White china group in C, brown shell on R, white
    shell on L, tall Chinese vase on L, round Chinese vase on R
  Top of bookshelves up R—Thin-necked vase in C, brown girl upstage, Dolphin
    candlestick downstage
  Fireplace, upstage end—*From top shelf downwards*—Teapot, girl with goat, girl
    with dog, brown streaked shell
    Downstage end—Flowered basket, white shell, girl with basket, metal figure
  In hall—Negro figure at foot of stairs holding vase with rushes
    Leaf table L of stairs with large blue vase
    Small tapestry chair
  Dining-room—Dining-table with bowl of fruit. Table laid for dinner

Off Stage R—Silver cigarette-case for CHARLES (EDITH)
  Tray with 5 cocktail glasses, 1 bottle of gin, 1 bottle of vermouth, a cocktail-
    shaker
  Ice-bucket with tongs for ice

At end of Scene 1—STRIKE
  Cocktail tray and glasses
  Ice-bucket
  MADAME ARCATI's cloak and bag

ACT I, Scene 2

SET: Coffee-tray (on writing-desk) with coffee-pot and milk-jug (silver),
  3 coffee-cups (MRS BRADMAN, RUTH and MADAME ARCATI)

CHECK: Records, cigarettes on piano, matches on mantelpiece

Off Stage R—Tray with whisky decanter, brandy decanter, whisky glasses, brandy glasses (1 whisky glass to break)

Doors open
Windows closed
Curtains ½ closed

At end of Scene 2—STRIKE
Coffee-tray and coffee-cups
Tray of drinks
Record off gramophone (re-set)
Re-set c table
Bowl of mixed flowers from piano

ACT II, SCENE 1

SET: Ashtray and silver box on c table
Breakfast-table (laid) LC
On breakfast-table—Checked cloth, 2 napkins, 2 cups and saucers, 2 small plates, 2 small knives, 1 large knife and fork, salt and pepper, glass jampot and spoon, sugar-basin, earthenware coffee-pot, and milk-jug
2 chairs from upstage R and down L
Copy of *The Times* on breakfast-table
Small vase of roses on breakfast-table
Vase of zinnias on writing-desk
Bowl of pansies on piano

Off Stage R—Tray with plate of bacon and eggs and toast-rack (EDITH)

Off Stage L—Bunch of grey roses (ELVIRA)

Curtains open
Upstage window open
Doors shut

At end of Scene—STRIKE
Clean rug
Breakfast-table
The Times
Table c
Grey roses and re-set zinnias
Roses in white vase from drinks table

ACT II, SCENE 2

SET: Small white table from downstage of piano to L end of sofa (cigarette-box off it goes on to piano)
On white table—Tray (silver) with 2 cups and saucers. Plate of cucumber sandwiches, sugar-basin, milk-jug, and tea-pot (all silver)
Dirty rug
The R side of door bolted
Doors shut
Windows shut
Curtains open
Re-set zinnias

At end of Scene—STRIKE
Dirty rug above sofa, with debris off tray
Bowl of pansies on piano
Vase of zinnias
Vase of red peonies

ACT II, SCENE 3

SET: Clean rug above sofa
  Re-set white table below piano with cigarette-box
  Re-set table c
  Tall glass vase of pink peonies on piano
  Green bowl of snapdragons on writing-desk
  Small tray with decanter of sherry and 4 glasses on drinks table upstage R
  Small bowl of roses on c table
CHECK: Telephone and sling for CHARLES

Doors shut
Windows shut
Curtains open

At end of Scene—STRIKE
  Vase of daisies from table downstage R
  Staffordshire figure on desk
  Tray of sherry from drinks table upstage R
  Small white table below piano

ACT III, SCENE 1

SET: Small white basket of daisies on table downstage R
  Move bowl of snapdragons from desk to drinks table upstage R
  Move silver cigarette-box from c table to desk
  Tray with whisky decanter, brandy decanter, brandy glasses, whisky glasses,
     syphon
  Cup of coffee and book for CHARLES

Doors shut
Curtains drawn
Window open, behind curtains

Off Stage—Salt-cellar and pepper-pot (CHARLES)

At end of Scene—STRIKE
  Salt-cellar and pepper-pot
  2 snapdragons on floor

ACT III, SCENE 2

SET: *On c table (now* LC)—Crystal, ouija board, 2 beer-mugs, playing cards,
     silver dish of sandwiches
  On floor below table—Loose playing-cards
  Re-set chair to below window
  Add two bottles of beer to drinks tray
CHECK: Cupid vase on mantelpiece and picture to fall off wall
  Branch of greenery above upstage curtain
  Branch of greenery above falling picture
  Branch of greenery above downstage R picture
  Branch of greenery above downstage R bracket
  Branch of greenery above on standard lamp pedestal
  Bunch of garlic above downstage L bracket
  Bunch of garlic on floor by window (cabalistic)
  Bunch of garlic on clock on mantelpiece
  Bunch of garlic against stone hearth
  Oak leaves on standard lamp

Off Stage R—Clock chimes
  White bandage (EDITH)
  Pound note (CHARLES)

Doors shut
Windows open behind curtains
Curtains drawn

THE LIGHTING PLOT
USED AT THE PICCADILLY THEATRE, LONDON

Floats—Two circuits: No. 3 amber and No. 36 pink
Batten No. 1—White, No. 3 amber, No. 4 amber, No. 36 pink
Battens 4 and 5—White, No. 3 amber, No. 36 pink
F.O.H.—Six 1,000 focus lamps, No. 3 amber
5 1,000 *Stage Floods.*—2 L, downstage at window
    1 upstage L
    1 upstage R
    1 upstage in dining-room backing (open white throughout)
2 1,000 *Standard Spots*—1 down stage, L, No. 21 green
    1 downstage, R, No. 21 green
Fire Spot.—Nos. 5, 7, 11
1 *Length* at top of stairs
1 *Length* on upstage of window flat   } all white throughout
1 *Length* on floor behind flower bank L
Pageant Sun Spot—L outside window (across breakfast-table), No. 4 amber
2 3-*Lamp brackets* on *stage*
1 standard lamp on stage
1 lamp on piano, on stage
1 desk lamp on stage
1 2-lamp bracket on stairs
2 electric fans L, outside window
1 wind machine upstage L

SETTING OF SPOT BATTEN

(Numbering from the R)

No. 1 36 pink on piano keyboard
No. 2 3 amber on piano keyboard
No. 3 3 amber on armchair
No. 4 36 pink on gramophone
No. 5 36 pink on breakfast-table
No. 6 36 pink on doorway
No. 7 36 pink on drinks table upstage R
No. 8 3 amber on mantelpiece
No. 9 3 amber on C table between sofa and armchair
No. 10 3 amber on lamp pedestal between bookcases
No. 11 36 pink on middle of sofa and downstage from it
No. 12 21 green on L arm of sofa (ELVIRA, end of Act I, Scene 2 only)

SETTING OF F.O.H.

Six lamps alternating upstage and downstage to cover whole of acting area

ACT I, SCENE 1

F.O.H.—No. 3 amber at *full*
Floats—No. 36 pink and No. 3 amber at *full*
Battens—No. 36 pink and No. 3 amber at *full*

Floods—L, downstage (window) Double 18 at $\frac{1}{2}$, No. 32 at $\frac{1}{2}$
  L and R, upstage, No. 36 pink at *full*
  Upstage flood in backing. Open white at *full*
Fire Spot (on to breakfast-table) at $\frac{3}{4}$
Staircase Length—On
Stage Brackets and Lamps—On
Spot Batten—All on except No. 12 at *full*
Cue 1 Fade in from blackout with rise
Cue 2 Fade out to blackout (working light)

ACT I, Scene 2

To open.—Some lighting as Scene 1
Cue 1 Fade in from blackout.
Cue 2 Snap out everything *except* desk lamp, fire spot, and window floods
Cue 3 Snap on
Cue 4 2 green spots (R and L downstage) on
Cue 5 Bring in No. 12 spot on batten and take out L green spot
Cue 6 Slow fade to blackout, bringing down green spots last (Houselights)

ACT II, Scene 1

F.O.H.—No. 3 amber to *full*
Floats—No. 36 pink and No. 3 amber to *full*
No. 1 Batten—All four circuits at *full*
Battens 4 and 5—White and No. 36 pink at *full*
Spot Batten—All on except No. 12 at *full*
Floods—L, downstage double 18 at *full*. Open white at *full*
  L and R, upstage No. 3 *amber* at *full*
Sun Spot—No. 4 amber at *full*
Stage Brackets and Lamps—Out
Staircase Length—On
L *Window Length*—On
Flower Bank Length—On
Fire Spot—On
Cue 1 Fade in from blackout with rise
Cue 2 Check sun spot slowly to out
Cue 3 L and R green spots on
Cue 4 Fade out to blackout (Working light)

ACT II, Scene 2

To open—Same lighting as Scene 1—*with*
  Window floods checked to $\frac{3}{4}$
  Sun spot out
  Green spots out
Cue 1 Fade in from blackout
Cue 2 Green spots on
Cue 3 Fade out to blackout (Working light)

ACT II, Scene 3

To open—Same lighting as Scene 2—*with*
  Window floods checked to $\frac{1}{2}$
  2 stage lamps on
  2 green spots off
Cue 1 Fade in from blackout

Cue 2   Green spots on
Cue 3   Green spots off
Cue 4   Green spots on
Cue 5   Fade out to blackout (Houselights)

ACT III, Scene 1

To open—Same lighting as Act I, Scene 1
Cue 1   Fade in from blackout
Cue 2   Green spots on
Cue 3   Same as Cue 2, Act I, Scene 2
Cue 4   Same as Cue 3, Act I, Scene 2
Cue 5   Blackout of everything on Master Switch (Working light)

ACT III, Scene 2

To open—Same lighting as Scene 1—with
   2 green spots on
   Fire spot off
Cue 1   Fade in from blackout (without fire)
Cue 2   Snap out (complete blackout)
   During blackout: Plug up sun spot
             Change L downstage flood from No. 32 to white (at *full*)
Cue 3   Snap in (all except window floods and sun spot)
Cue 4   Snap in window floods and sun spot

SAMUEL FRENCH STAFF

Nate Collins
President

Ken Dingledine
Director of Operations,
Vice President

Bruce Lazarus
Executive Director,
General Counsel

Rita Maté
Director of Finance

ACCOUNTING

Lori Thimsen | Director of Licensing Compliance
Nehal Kumar | Senior Accounting Associate
Charles Graytok | Accounting and Finance Manager
Glenn Halcomb | Royalty Administration
Jessica Zheng | Accounts Receivable
Andy Lian | Accounts Payable
Charlie Sou | Accounting Associate
Joann Mannello | Orders Administrator

BUSINESS AFFAIRS

Caitlin Bartow | Assistant to the Executive Director

CORPORATE COMMUNICATIONS

Abbie Van Nostrand | Director of Corporate
Communications

CUSTOMER SERVICE AND LICENSING

Brad Lohrenz | Director of Licensing Development
Laura Lindson | Licensing Services Manager
Kim Rogers | Theatrical Specialist
Matthew Akers | Theatrical Specialist
Ashley Byrne | Theatrical Specialist
Jennifer Carter | Theatrical Specialist
Annette Storckman | Theatrical Specialist
Julia Izumi | Theatrical Specialist
Sarah Weber | Theatrical Specialist
Nicholas Dawson | Theatrical Specialist
David Kimple | Theatrical Specialist
Ryan McLeod | Theatrical Specialist

EDITORIAL

Amy Rose Marsh | Literary Manager
Ben Coleman | Literary Associate

MARKETING

Ryan Pointer | Marketing Manager
Courtney Kochuba | Marketing Associate
Chris Kam | Marketing Associate

PUBLICATIONS AND PRODUCT DEVELOPMENT

Joe Ferreira | Product Development Manager
David Geer | Publications Manager
Charlyn Brea | Publications Associate
Tyler Mullen | Publications Associate
Derek P. Hassler | Musical Products Coordinator
Zachary Orts | Musical Materials Coordinator

OPERATIONS

Casey McLain | Operations Supervisor
Elizabeth Minski | Office Coordinator, Reception
Coryn Carson | Office Coordinator, Reception

SAMUEL FRENCH BOOKSHOP (LOS ANGELES)

Joyce Mehess | Bookstore Manager
Cory DeLair | Bookstore Buyer
Kristen Springer | Customer Service Manager
Tim Coultas | Bookstore Associate
Bryan Jansyn | Bookstore Associate
Alfred Contreras | Shipping & Receiving

LONDON OFFICE

Anne-Marie Ashman | Accounts Assistant
Felicity Barks | Rights & Contracts Associate
Steve Blacker | Bookshop Associate
David Bray | Customer Services Associate
Robert Cooke | Assistant Buyer
Stephanie Dawson | Amateur Licensing Associate
Simon Ellison | Retail Sales Manager
Robert Hamilton | Amateur Licensing Associate
Peter Langdon | Marketing Manager
Louise Mappley | Amateur Licensing Associate
James Nicolau | Despatch Associate
Emma Anacootee-Parmar | Production/Editorial
Controller
Martin Phillips | Librarian
Panos Panayi | Company Accountant
Zubayed Rahman | Despatch Associate
Steve Sanderson | Royalty Administration Supervisor
Douglas Schatz | Acting Executive Director
Roger Sheppard | I.T. Manager
Debbie Simmons | Licensing Sales Team Leader
Peter Smith | Amateur Licensing Associate
Garry Spratley | Customer Service Manager
David Webster | UK Operations Director
Sarah Wolf | Rights Director

SAMUELFRENCH.COM
SAMUELFRENCH-LONDON.CO.UK